"Country Matters ͻͻ-
rary and nostalgi͏ e
novel unlike any ͻnt
in the pre-rock 19͏
Watergate 1970s, it captivates—sexy, saucy, witty, and senti-
mental. We follow a group of high school friends as they
grow out of their Midwest and make their way East, only to
find that they can never escape passions and loves, both
consummated and unrequited, of their adolescence.
Osander's style is imaginative and evocative, shifting
frames of reference, lending delicate shadings and raunchy
humor. You will end up rooting for Joe and Amy, Mickey
and Kathy, even as they frustrate and enthrall. This is an
important work by an author who creates a world you
remember and characters you will never forget."
—**Landon Jones**—*People* magazine,
former managing editor
*Great Expectations: America and
the Baby Boom Generation*

"It's about roads not taken and the ache of young love. It's
about teenage swimming parties, long talks on the dock,
secrets shared by best girlfriends and a hidden wish list."
—**Mary Ann Grossmann**—Book Editor,
Saint Paul Pioneer Press

"An astonishing book! This acrostic of layered memories
must have been rewritten and rewritten, unlike the boring,
linear stuff of convention. It gets the right tone with an
appropriately sassy interplay of annotation and story-
telling. A spectacular book."
—**Hugh Hardy, FAIA**
—Designer of Minneapolis Orchestra Hall,
Restorator of Radio City Music Hall
and Ford's Theater

"A thrilling ride back to the innocence of youth and a whole New World for those who haven't been there. Osander's *Country Matters* reads like a lost F. Scott Fitzgerald novel, filled with characters straight out of our own adolescence. The author's flair for words made me laugh, then cry, and somehow, I want to go back and do it all over again."
—**John Koblas**—*The Jesse James Northfield Raid, Willow River Almanac, Selected Letters of Sinclair Lewis, F. Scott Fitzgerald in Minnesota*

"Fabulous! It thrilled me."
—**Sarah Tantillo**—Executive Director, New Jersey Charter Schools

"Faulkner wrote, 'The past is never dead. It isn't even past.' With vivid and bittersweet visions—achingly real, beautifully accurate—Osander deftly portrays how the past shapes us irrevocably for the journey ahead, and how young, fresh, enchanted encounters with life remain with us always whether we cling to them or not."
—**Stanley G. West**—*Until They Bring the Streetcars Back, Amos, Finding Laura Buggs*

"This is a wonderful period piece that captures the 50's era—both the inner and outer lives of teenagers and young adults. The language, issues, and characters bring us right back to the pain, misfortunes, and thrills of the times—historically and developmentally. I look forward to seeing it on more than the printed page."
—**Marsha H. Levy-Warren, Ph.D.**—*The Adolescent Journey: Development, Identity Formation, and Psychotherapy*

"A fine story, told with much energy and a great eye for detail, that captures the era as well as the frenetic and frantic world of teens."

—George H. Gallup, Jr.—
Chairman of Gallup International Institute,
The Gallup Poll Public Opinion: Cumulative Index 1935-1997,
The Next American Spirituality: Finding God in the Twenty-
First Century, What Teens Really Think

"A beautiful story, beautifully told. I found myself immensely moved, and smiled, laughed, nodded in agreement, and shed an occasional tear. It shows how terribly, achingly difficult it is to maintain the feeling of magical intimacy that accompanies all new love."

—Don Larson
—Professor, Romance Languages, Ohio State

"The writing has the ease and fluidity of great narratives and the unique twist needed in good contemporary literature. A humorous story filled with descriptive language, compelling action, and bizarre storyline."

—Anton Mueller—NYC fiction editor

"The future of fiction: we have entered the age of 'The Novel With Footnotes.'"

—Margaret Johnson—*The Daily Princetonian,*
Princeton University

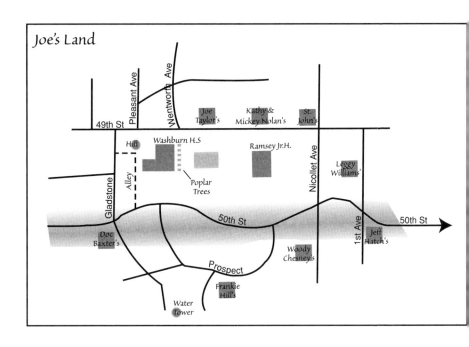

Joe's Land

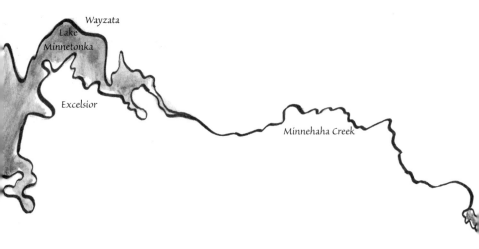

South
Minneapolis

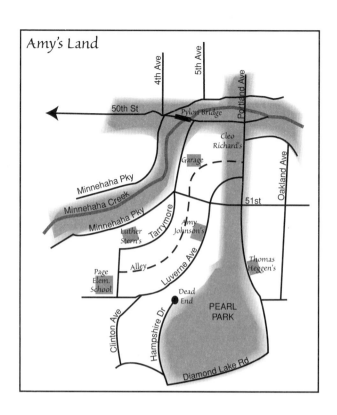

Amy's Land

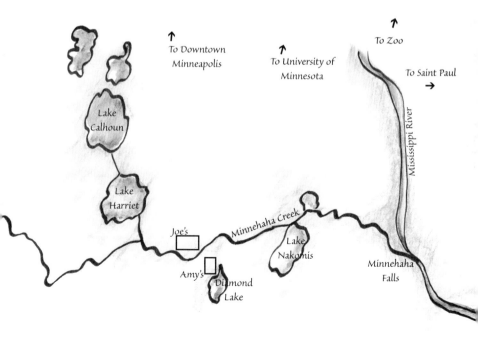

Country Matters

Narrative and Commentary on
Joseph Taylor Jr.'s Early 1950s Journal
As Reconstructed by Close Friends
Kathryn Nolan & ~~Michael Nolan~~ Mickey N

John Osander

Beaver's Pond Press, Inc.
Edina,   Minnesota

Ellen,
Thanks. You might
be the youngest
reader so far. We
almost over-lapped at WHS.
Were you in 9th at Ramsey
in '53. Now HS = 9-12.
Best,
John Osander
Jack

ISBN 1-890676-98-5

Library of Congress Catalog Number: 2001087895

First printed in hardcover in November 2000
First softcover printing, February 2001

Printed in the United States of America.

04 03 02 01   5 4 3 2 1

A Half Century Ago with Author (JO)…

Not so long ago Minneapolis built a public library at 53rd and Lyndale where, sixty years ago when four, I'd walk two blocks to wait….

I've been fortunate, over half a century, finding collaborators—living *and dead*: Blue, Chiarella, Doucette, Dowell, Eaton, Gesner, Glassco, *Lyon*, *Stewart*…Covey, Cruz, Forman, Friedman, Porterfield, Price, Rawls, Tantillo, Weidlein….

Minneapolis 2000

JO[1]

[1.] MN: (Michael "Mickey" Nolan) Who the fuck's "Author (JO)"?

KN: (Kathryn "Kathy" Nolan) Watch the foul tonguing, twit twin.

MN: Never heard of no JO at Washburn and he's no character in the Journal. I oughta know. I found it. Blue, no key, busted lock. And I reconstructed the mutha.

KN: I…okay, *we*…reconstructed…Joe's Journal!

MN: But that crap up there! This page flew in from Yawnsville, man. No first names. And calling JO the Author? Snake shit on that!

KN: What's up there is all I could remember from the full page.

MN: Full page? What Mister Beaver P. mailed us?

KN: Did you toss it? Listen, Lesser Half: Beaver's Pond Press is our publisher; JO, one of their people. And he wants to have his say about the early '50s. So where did you toss his page?

MN: Floor probably.

KN: Find it! *If* you want them to publish Joe's Journal.

MN: That's black-fuckin'-mail.

KN: Well at least JO didn't scratch his name in large letters under the title. We *have* to include his "Half Century" Page. Let's put it *after* Joe's story. Now what do we do with JO's didactic little essay: "School and Neighborhood in the Early '50s"?

MN: Cut some! Stuff the rest between scenes. That'll give Joe and Amy a chance to come up for air. All they fuckin' do is talk and make-out. Nothing go-fast like your twin's revelation one chapter from the end.

KN: What reader will believe that? Anyway I get the book's last line.

MN: So we cram JO's crap into vaudeville patters. What say, Miss Sugar Square?

KN: I'll play along. Now let's get to our Joe. (If you're impatient and need to understand the title now, try Footnote 72, Page 190. Do that and you can start and finish the book in minutes.) Turn this page and you'll find Hamlet in court.

MN: In court? Hell your guy Hamlet's trying to lay in his girl's lap.

KN: Turn the page!

He: Lady, shall I lie in your lap?
She: No, my lord.
He: I mean my head upon your lap?
She: Ay, my lord.
He: Do you think I meant country matters? [2]

Fall 1950

Joe plunges down another stairway. Sophomore new, likely late for last period class, he rushes by a blur, hardly hearing clicks behind him. At the bottom he turns to find himself facing Room 003. Wrong!

He wants 103 for geometry. Feeling his father's white shirt getting even damper, he pivots and races back up, now noticing ahead loafers with metal wedges sunk in the backs of a girl's small heels. Also a flash of leg and floating blue skirt. He steps left to avoid a crash, his shirt scraping plaster. The girl from sophomore homeroom with the sleeveless blouse and all those crinolines stays ahead of him. Reaching the landing, he hears distant flag pulleys chiming against their pole.

Even though the tardy bell has stopped ringing, he slows to study the straw ponytail and scar on the girl's throat. She doesn't look at him, but turns where the stairway turns and, holding her books against her chest, continues up. She keeps going without even a "Hi!"—hunching her shoulders so he can't steal a look, the way he tries in homeroom. Not hearing lockers as they clang from hall to hall, Joe watches with awe as she reaches the main floor and braces her books against the

---

2. KN: Know, Joe, that I voted against this. Several times! Against touching your Journal. But when my dim twin found it, he proclaimed, "We must expand it!" (Some of your blue Journal was sentences, but some only notes or outline that really *did* need filling in.) And *we* of course turned out to mean *I*. Know too that I did slice some words Mickey slipped in. Then I put them back, because I had slipped in a few too.

banister with a hip. She unfastens an elastic binder and tosses
her hair, then very coolly finger combs and winds it back to
reshape her pony tail. As she disappears into the voices
toward the 50th Street doors, Joe Taylor dries his hands on dull
gray corduroys, sure of one thing about Amy Johnson: her
mouth makes Washburn High's finest pout.

After class Joe pulls a sweater over his damp shirt before
the new girl, who moved up from Richmond over the summer, corners toward him from the 49th Street doors. He can't
believe she's standing as close as she is to draw a serpentine in
the air that ends with her finger tap on his chest. In spite of
what several soph girls including Kathy Nolan say, Joe's not
bothered by Carrie Browne's slightly "elevated" style. She's
one of the few who often wears long stockings to school,
seams straight as streetcar tracks under anklets turned down
above white bucks less scuffed than most. And those polished
tan arms! Carrie Browne brings summer into September when
she drawls, "Walk me to the game? They say South High's
here and I don't know a soul! Really! Not a living Midwestern
soul, hear?"[3]

3. KN: That sweet fresh thing from the far Commonwealth of Virginia
       hadn't learned to drawl "Midwest." Or more precisely "Upper
       Midwest," the terrific name the winner came up with in the
       Minneapolis *Star-Journal* and *Tribune* contest.
  MN: "Midwestern" was a furnace factory on Hennepin Island.
  KN: Carrie moved north the summer Joe was emerging from that
       cocoon designed to diminish junior high boys. Now there he is:
       ready to face girls. Sorta!
  MN: He had to fat fuckin' face you since kindergarten.
  KN: Okay, but please don't say, "You had your chance."
  MN: Won't say that, but gotta say I just *do not* understand it.
  KN: You don't understand what?
  MN: That whole fuckin' footnote before Page 1—the whole JO "Half-
       Century" Page. It ain't ever gonna make sense.
  KN: Some of it's you talking.
  MN: I did some talking while you sat there writing who knows what.
       And you kept reading me version after version. How am I sup-
       posed to know what it means?
  KN: Go back and read it again! And again!

⌒

From his seat high in the bleachers Joe hears the punch of black gym shoes behind him, springing from the mesh and bouncing higher. "No big deal," he tells Carrie. "It's only Mickey. Old foul-mouthed-do-nothing climbs that fence instead of doing homework."

"Someone's chasing him," Carrie says. "I can't see who through the poplars."

"No big deal." Joe concentrates on the luck of having the new girl next to him. He thinks she may have nudged closer on the splintery board.

"It's Mickey's sister. From all the talk I imagined you and Kathy always sat together."

"No problem! I told her I'd buy tickets, but she'll get in. We've seen a billion games since kindergarten; she won't mind."[4]

"I wouldn't want her to think I moved all the way north to act 'inappropriate.'" Carrie slides her sweater up glassy, tan arms, seemingly immune to autumn coolness.

Down near the field the "in-group" Soph girls—those with not-so-badly-blemished chins—crowd close, yelling and waving bees away from their caramel apples. South High moves the ball well with their single wing. Joe's buddy Doc Baxter, the only Soph who made varsity, stands with an assistant coach who wraps an arm around Doc's pads. He gestures toward the field with jerky fingers as though Doc might get his

---

[4]   KN: Mickey sees this reconstruction of your Journal, Joe—which of course he hasn't read—as a friendly gesture. I see it as my effort to accept what really happened. So consider it the Joe Taylor, Jr. story translated by a Generous Asshole and a Never-Blooming Non-Beauty. When Mickey declared, "Let's open with a blast of horns," well I didn't buy that, at first. Then I figured, well why not? Let's position Princess Amy (with Leggy, Cleo, Carrie—*and me*) in front of a paint-peeling backdrop. Let's march in procession with Ophelia, Juliet, Psyche, Cressida, Leda: a cosmic procession of teen belles.

   MN: Finest kind! Find costumes and toss in Venus and Jayne Mansfield. Forget the costumes but come up with some hot Svear Beauty. Good Midwest Swede stock for old Joe to shack up with.

first chance to call signals. In the stands the girl from home-room with the throat scar licks cotton candy from her wrist.

Teachers patrol to keep kids from sneaking over the fence: twelve feet, topped by three strands of outward-pointing barbed wire. Mickey rebounds to grab the top wires, reaching to lock an elbow on a poplar branch. "Fasten your seat belts jockey worshippers." He pushes off the tree and swings easily above the barbs across the four-foot gap between fence and bleachers. "Make room! A fine fuckin' fan's finally here. Gimme the score?" Mickey bumps a bunch of juniors to push for a place by Joe and Carrie. He pulls his Hathaway Man patch over his red head to cover one eye. "No ripped balls or pissed-on pants this trip. So how they hangin', Joe baby? Three in a cluster or two in a bunch? Wait! Don't tell us till Kathy gets here; she'll want to know. Look at her: bent over dragging a case of that new Clearasil crap across the grass. They use that down south, Browne?"

"How did you get over that fence so easily?" Carrie asks, smoothing where the wind has ruffled her straight ash blond hair.

"All the neighborhood kids, boys *and* girls, learn to scale that fence," Joe says. "And any kid can wiggle through the hole along 49th across from my house and the Nolan's."

Mr. G., the assistant principal, winds along the row of poplars that runs end zone to end zone. Kathy times her move until he passes, then runs to where Mickey went over. Mr. G. blends into the foliage near her. A pop bottle shatters against the tree where he hides.

Joe's now sure that Carrie's pressing her leg against his. He hopes someone notices. Especially the "in-group" girls. Most admit that Carrie's smart and can dance the fast stuff even in heels. Some envy her for a chest that ranks high in boy-talk competitions. A few, like Kathy, dislike the way she "Honey's" the guys and rattles her charm bracelet to attract attention when she raises her hand in class.

Mr. G. emerges from his tree. Seen by students as Hitler's narcotic-eyed "Goebbels," he creeps toward Kathy, who abruptly makes her move. Slamming her toes in the mesh, she goes for a grip.

Her feet are smaller and fit more easily than her twin brother's, but her loafers slip as she climbs hand over hand. At the top she bounces to find a poplar branch for balance. With both feet outside the barbed strands, she looks across the space at her brother, and at Joe—with Carrie Browne.

In the lower stands, puffs float from girls' mouths. In the chill air Joe can't tell for sure who's really smoking, but his belly flips as he spots the profile of straw ponytail. Outside the fence an ice-sucking rasp shouts, "Out of the tree!" Between the gray boards Joe sees Kathy's feet on the fence, not out of reach if Mr. G. were to sacrifice dignity and go up on his toes. "I want your name young lady. Tell me her name! That redhead. Someone tell me her name!"

The Miller cheerleaders, wearing white sweaters with blue "W's" topping orange skirts that ride above their knees when they leap, yell, "Lean to the left; lean to the right." Doc Baxter pulls down his helmet.[5] A South half-

---

5. MN: When we were in Ramsey, the Washburn coach came to watch Doc bullet balls that knocked the wind out of his junior high receivers. The coach watched him loft passes forty yards into an end's open belly, when one of them could run fast enough to get that far downfield. But Kath?

   KN: You're interrupting me. Look, Joe's Journal's stranded me up on this fence.

   MN: Well, I did look back at that first footnote and still don't understand it. Too many names.

   KN: Go back and *study* it. If a professor were teaching this book in a course, she'd suggest that you know that page cold before a final exam. To *understand* the book, you *have* to understand the relationships among the characters. It's all there in that note. I worked hard to get it down to 32 lines. Would you rather I'd written an essay?

   MN: Who reads footnotes anyway? Or that small type with poems and stuff writers put in the middle of books. People skip right over that.

   KN: If they skip the notes in this, they're going to miss half the story—if I say so myself. *Our* part! And *you* better be funny!

   MN: I guess that is where I get to talk. But it's blackmail to have to cram in some other guy's junk. Bush League! So tell me what "Country Matters" means.

   KN: Maybe when you're older—or later in the book. I told you it's coming on page 190. I'll give you a hint: it's Elizabethan vulgar.

   MN: I can't wait to hear the dirty details.

back pitches out for a first down. Cheerleaders snap their movements; girls in the stands lean against each other, loose-limbed, hair tangled by the breeze. Joe follows the swing of straw.

Math whiz Luther Stern stretches what he can of his 210 pounds across the gap from bleachers to poplars. He can only reach Kathy's elbow, but holds on while she lifts one loafer and positions it inside, straddling the wires.

Mickey shouts, "Clear her a spot!"

Joe swivels to slide up the stands so he can lay his chest over the top rail. Luther holds him around the waist. Carrie and Mickey each grab a leg as Joe tries to get closer. His hand grips Kathy's inside ankle, but her far arm clings tight to the tree. "Come on!" he calls. Kathy looks across and slowly places a second foot inside the barbs, letting go of Luther to wrap one hand around the top wire while the other still clings to a branch.

Joe tries to steady both ankles. Mr. G. turns his back to the fence. His fingers begin to play the mesh like a harp until it moves.

Kathy holds even tighter and will not let go of the tree enough to take Joe's outstretched hand, as she stands above the protective bridge of his body.

Joe feels Luther's meaty hands locking tighter as he watches Kathy's loafers teeter on the narrow metal. Goebbels, who remains facing away from the fence, fingers pulsating until the fence sways, rasps, "I could call a cop."

"You *are* a cop!" Carrie calls down. Joe's fingers tremble. He cannot lift Kathy across, and Carrie and Luther can barely keep him pressed into the stands. Each time Joe stretches, barbs dig and drag deeper into his chest.

A roar from the far side signals a South High touchdown, but some of the sophomore girls have turned away from the field to look toward the fence top.

Mickey looks across at his sister. "Okay, bend so those knock knees level with the top strand. Then all ya gotta do is twist and push off from the tree. Hard! Then dance across Taylor's shoulders. Okay?"

Kathy slowly lets go of the branch, bending her knees while bringing her trailing hand to the wire. The swaying fence snaps. She lets go, raking an ankle over the wires as she grabs for the tree with both hands.

Joe leans as far out as he can without losing his balance, belly on the barbs, feeling Carrie and Mickey hanging like hounds on his legs. "Here. Take it," he tries to say calmly. "You're okay. Step over like you did before and just fall toward us. I'll worry about your legs. Just let go."

The fence sways again, then stops. Joe keeps his grip on her ankles. Kathy stands suspended. She rises above the fence with one foot on each side of the barbwire, her hands no longer holding anything. Then a leather sole slips.

As her hand slaps at leaves, the fence whips and her body drops. From wrist to shoulder, groin to ankle, she's dragged across barbs as she falls headfirst through the foliage to the concrete.

Carrie doesn't hear the cheer from across the field as she pushes through the crowd to get down the bleachers, ripping her sweater into strips as she runs to the foot of the fence. Mickey follows, holding the sides of Kathy's face: motionless, colorless. Doc drops his helmet and runs to tuck his warm-up jacket around Kathy and keep people away. Luther stays in the stands with Joe, easing him on his back to see how badly his body has been ripped.

Luther looks toward Carrie and Doc huddled over Kathy. Joe raises his head enough to see Amy Johnson drop her caramel apple between the boards onto the concrete. Mr. G. , hands folded behind his back like a long-distance skater, strolls toward the opposite end zone.

∽

Off their private point below Carrie's cottage on the bluff, Joe wades in the chill waves of Excelsior Bay. Kathy sits, her hip-to-toe plaster cast blending with rocks to form a sculpted seat. "Listen!" she says. "That's a Pontiac with problems."

A decaying maple branch bobs into a crevice, lapped by a wave that sprays their legs. Joe splashes below her rock. She listens and looks across the bay to the amusement park where four years ago they rode buses to their 6th grade picnic. They watch the ferris wheel and count pinwheels. Down the shore a mistroked paddle slaps against canoe canvas, echoing. The park and night sky dazzle.

On the bluff the second soph bash of the fall swings in the Browne cottage. When Carrie moved north her father said, "Make friends! Invite them out. We won't use the cottage that much."

Kathy labels it, "instant popularity," as she fishes a painkiller from her pocket, having waited until she hurts more than she should. "A sound commercial venture by Browne, Inc."

"Carrie fit in real fast," Joe says. "She's sharp and not a bad looker."

"She works at that. But I'm being bitchy. She *is* naturally attractive *and* well groomed—given that she only has a few closets to work with. Sorry! Stop me when I start that. I won't forget how you stuck your neck—hell, half your body or more—out and got cut up for me. I'm hardly the only girl dragging around a little plaster from an accidental fall. Carrie *does* dance well."

Joe picks up one of Kathy's crutches and takes a left-handed cut like Ted Williams. "It's natural to be pissed off. That was *not* an accident."

"Well, when I *could* get around and offered to teach you to dance, you turned me down—real fast. Try Carrie!"

"That would turn me off real fast."

"I thought you liked the flattery. And the drawl. You let her drool all over your locker."[6]

"Maybe at first," Joe says. "But she bubbles too much and her music's dumb."

"Are you suggesting that 'Lavender Blue' didn't deserve to top the charts? Even though it dropped from the Top Ten they played it Saturday as a Lucky Strike Extra. Or am I confusing it with 'Zip Up Your Doo Dah'?"

"Now they're playing that guy with the hearing aid squealing about his crying cloud."

"*White cloud!*" Kathy whips her head from water to woods. "There! You must have heard that motor? It's a car, but definitely not the fuzz."

"At first Carrie was okay. Now she makes me cloyed."

"Try her 'cloyedness' or 'cloyingness.' Worth points on your College Boards. And, yes, that is the Carrie we've all gotten to know. Your cloying little girlfriend."

Joe rakes the lower branches of an oak with the crutch so a shower of crusty leaves forces Kathy to scuttle backwards on the rocks. "She's *not* my girlfriend—even though Mickey

---

6. KN: Joe wasn't sure what to make of Carrie always at his locker. The Browne girl brought her campaign north, surveyed the field, and declared herself in unrelenting, overt pursuit of the quite attainable—until after this soph party at her cottage—Joe Taylor.
MN: And what about that nice Nolan girl?
KN: She was never enough rebel. Too solidly Midwest: Sturdy Swede Svear. And her locks were too orange.
MN: Well Carrie let you know she was there. I heard she always wore long sleeves to cover thick, brown arm hairs. Until she read an article in *Photoplay* and accepted her hirsute kinship with Liz Taylor and Monty Clift. But when she pictured herself in a swimsuit in one of our 10,000 lakes, she submitted to the procedure.
KN: "Hypertrichosis." Painful! Performed by a trichologist.
MN: Her arms got as smooth as if she shaved every time she brushed her teeth.
KN: She asked Joe to the Sadie Hawkins dance then erected that tent by his locker, a floor below hers, and managed to run into him enroute to every class. She waited for him to ask her out.
MN: And waited! And waited!
KN: Just like me!

said he wouldn't kick her out of his bunk for tracking in sand. I don't *have* a girlfriend!"[7]

"Maybe you will by Halloween. If not, at least you won't get sidetracked by infatuation. If you go east to Princeton you can write for the Triangle Club, and then who knows—a Broadway show?"

"Ya, that's me. Famous as hell, but *not* in a college out East," Joe says.

"That is definitely a Pontiac with a hood gasket about to go."

A firefly lights on each side of him and Joe tries to catch one in his fist. "Carburetors can gleam like butterflies."

"Heavens, little fellow!" Kathy snorts "From which crackerjack box did you pull that? Repeat that in gym, and the big boys will yank your jock to your ankles. That would make the girls laugh."

"Amy? Would she laugh?"

"She might not notice."

Cars roll onto sand roads in the woods. No headlights. Doors creak. Shadowy silhouettes snap branches, loud like cherry bombs. Joe says, "Move over! I want up on that rock."

"Whatever you need."

"If you're planning to limp away on water, don't! The lake's as cold as gym showers."

"Same as the girls'. Our showers pee ice cubes."

"I can't imagine actually being inside a girls' locker room."

"Oh, I bet you can. Girls haven't changed much since 6th grade. We kid more about boys' privates, their size and shape. But we agree that all girls look pretty much the same. Am I embarrassing you? You know what good sport, Kathy,

---

7. KN: I simply tried to point Joe toward three things: 1) studying to go East to college, 2) preparing for his significant destiny, 3) holding to good Midwest Middle Class Values. Jeff Hatch had already nailed the first two and didn't care about the third because of his capacity to attract girls. Joe thought he wanted that.

MN: Your "Big Three"? I'm not sure you sold those. And though I don't read much, I *did* go back and try Footnote 1 again. How many times do I have to try that before it makes sense? And I noticed Footnote 2—about you slicing out my words and then putting them back. What words? Where do I find them and how can I be sure they're back?

Basketball Sub Number One, did? When Carrie moved from Richmond, I moved to the bench, right next to Amy. She said, 'It's okay, I'm here.' And you know what I said? I said, 'Shit, Amy, you *always* sit here!' Nice, huh?"[8]

Using the crutch Joe works his way up and wedges himself on the chain of rocks next to Kathy. She presses her cheek against his chest. They hold hands without fumbling, a lock between friends who have lived three houses apart since kindergarten. They don't move even when the best sky display of the night explodes. For years they've rested like this after rolling and wrestling on every lush slope on the Ramsey and Washburn grounds.

Mosquito humming blends with lapping seaweed and foam. Above, Carrie's three-speed Webcor changer blares as it drops a new set of 45 RPMs, which someone else will soon stack in a different order. Kathy says, "Sometimes I want to do something so wrong. Do you ever feel that way, slugger?"

"Not if anyone's looking."

"I don't know if I can take three more years of all this sameness. I want the East and Wellesley or Bryn Mawr. I'll settle for Pembroke if I get too many 'B's' for talking back in class."

"Why not the U with the rest of us?"

"Same group? Talk about the same things? Maybe a mention of Benny Goodman, but never Ralph Bunche or Matisse. No notice of Alger Hiss or Klaus Fuchs. No, I'd rather run into a band of strangers come to pillage and ravish the Miller maidens."

"Yeah, your mom would love learning about that. Mothers are big on strange ravishers."

"She's a doll and we talk a lot, but she works too late too often. She'd never know and dad's not around to beat me up the way he did Mickey."

"Your dad did look like John Wayne, only smaller and probably not so strong."

"He was strong enough to kick the shit out of Mickey— even though my brother usually deserved it."

---

8. MN: Since 7th grade at Ramsey, everyone knew the shy ones. But confident guys like Jeff Hatch, veteran of tennis locker rooms, with his thick left-leaning member, could act oblivious about packing twice the gear of other sophomores. But at least no one pointed and laughed at Joe—or me.

"What would these strangers pillage?"

"I'm not sure they'd see anything to pillage, let alone ravage. But what if they did and what if I liked it? What if I found them kind and gentle?"

"I don't think gangs practice sharpening their 'kind and gentle.'"

A pinwheel splits and splatters. Kathy says, "I haven't ridden that rickety roller coaster since the girl from Roosevelt fell, and I've never been keen on the Fun House. You creeps gawk when that dirty old man blows his wind machine up our skirts. But over here on our point of rocks—how's this?—we possess beams sprinkled by the moon on the backs of silent sunfish."

Suddenly bright lights blaze across the water. Joe jumps from the rocks to the sand as headlights bathe the bay. He calls back to Kathy, "Better put your solo loafer on so—how's this?—some silent sunfish doesn't nibble your good foot."

Revved-up voices hoot and tease as boys—some they recognize, some they don't—pile from cars. Some boys peer through the brush; some walk the sand; some wade in. Kathy swings her crutches to follow over the uneven shore.

A dozen yards out girls' bodies huddle, trembling in the glare. Too few hands fumble to cover too much. A brown head ducks in the shallows. Kathy says, "That's Leggy laughing it off." Doc and others from the cottage dash down the steps, Luther at the rear.[9]

---

9. MN: Did you say? Klaus Fuchs?
KN: That's right.
MN: Up to him, I guess. Anyway, seventh grade Phys. Ed. for boys was the worst. But even then the teacher stayed away from state tennis champ Jeff Hatch. Instead he'd stand face-to-face with Luther Stern, pinching his arm and belly. "If we could trim you down, you might be just what we need to take a beating in the center of the line. Don't all 'A's' mean you know left from right?"
"Yes, Sir," Luther answered.
"And you're—'Goldstern'?"
"Just 'Stern, Sir.'"
"Okay, gentlemen, I want one line. Hands on waists—place! I don't want to see any fingers hunting for nuts in your shorts. You too, Stern. This isn't history class."
KN: Jolly Luther complained when his little sister started to latch the bathroom door because she didn't want her big brother to see her pop a pimple. Luther groaned, "I don't care what she does in there, but a guy's gotta take a leak sometime."
MN: And of course Luther took longer because he had to roll his shriveled dick out from under his fat gut.

Leggy Williams bobs up squirting water through her palms. "You guys horny?" Leggy shouts as she straightens and splashes her naked 5' 11" to shore. Most of the boys step away as she strides past, as casual as when she returns to the bench to pull on her sweats after practice.

Another tall girl reaches the woods farther down shore where she takes a towel from a tree and tucks it from her breasts to her knees: Carrie Browne, ash blond hostess. Joe has to admire that chest, as he admires how she can dribble on a court or walk a hallway, head motionless, eyes keeping contact until—with a flick—she breaks for the basket, invites herself along for burgers, or explains the harmonies of the universe.

Before picking up her shorts and shirt Leggy wipes down her legs the way she waxes skis. More modest, Carrie retucks her towel. Cleo Richards wades to shore but can't find her clothes so bums a cigarette from Luther. Most of the boys from other schools drift back through the woods. Kathy looks up and down the beach to see she's the only girl who's really dressed, even if she does wear only one shoe.

"You FEMS form such an attractive cluster," Carrie says. "It must be great going back that many years. But wait. One of you is missing."[10]

"A lot of laughs," Leggy says. "One winter we lost Cleo in a snowdrift."

"Someone always drowns when we have a party," Cleo says, pulling up her shorts and lighting a cigarette.

[10.] MN: Soph boys never could beat the competition. There you were: the famous FEMS from Page School: you, Leggy, and Cleo. Did I count right?

KN: You forgot Amy. FEMS means FOUR.

MN: Imagine that? I forgot Amy. Well it was no thrill watching all the junior and senior guys coming over to our house to see *your* friends when no girls paid attention to us. I suppose some even came to see you.

KN: Thanks a heap! A big big bunch of heap.

MN: Heap's cheap!

KN: Creep!

"You're so funny, Leggy," Carrie says. "And you, Kathy. So many brains and all that wackiness."

"Wackiness?"

"Sharp and funny! You read and remember everything." Carrie's eyes sweep the sand. "Someone *is* missing."

Leggy says to Cleo, "I understand you're going to the movies with Jeff Hatch this weekend."

"Yeah, do you mind?"

"Why would I mind?"

"I think he's a very nice boy," Cleo declares.

"Keep your legs together."

From high in an overhanging willow Mickey wails so loudly he scares the guy across the bay on the ferris wheel about to put his hand under his girl's skirt.

"Oh, God," Leggy says. "Can't someone give the kid movie money to go away?"

Mickey swings out, drops, and splashes. He points deeper into the lake. They all look at the girl, mostly underwater except her face, hair dripping over her ears like honey.

Until she stands, shakes her ponytail, and comes toward them, no one moves. She stops, neither ducking nor running for the woods, defiantly refusing to angle her elbows to cover herself.

As car motors clack, her eyes flatten. She holds her mouth tight, eyes darting: a creature who senses danger but will forget as soon as it passes.

"God," Leggy says, "Check out the Princess! The beauty of a young Goddess! Eyes of a soaked vixen! A temptress? You bet she is, though I don't think she knows it yet."

"She pouts better than anyone," Cleo says.

"When she's pissed off," Kathy says. "Usually it's just the way she holds her lips; she's not really sulky—that often."

Joe sees a shine below the girl's waist. He's not sure whether it's silk or skin. He sees a dusky patch between her hips, which disappears each time a wave washes her.

As though calling for a fair catch, Amy from homeroom flicks aside her ponytail and raises a hand toward the fireworks and the stars. Joe forgets the others sloshing or pulling on clothes. He picks up a rotting stick and lobs it toward her. A life preserver. She doesn't grab but bats so the wood disintegrates and dusts her shoulders and hair.

Joe and the girl remain alone inside a warm tunnel. Alone there until he feels a sharp slap on his back. Kathy!

"Sorry to break it to you, Joe baby, but that's one picture of the Johnson Princess you won't see in our yearbook."[11]

[11.] MN: See how fast Amy snowed Joe?

KN: Oh, I suppose she did.

MN: Suppose, madam?

KN: Oh, get lost, Bug. Hey, Joe. I hope you hear more joy from our romantic punchbowl of the 50s, than drips from our acid notes looking back from the next century. But over that time I've learned a powerful truth. Don't include Juliet and her guy. And I'm probably hurting my own case by mentioning this right at the time you began to feel, well, "infatuated" by Amy. But most teens possess a power to love too serious to be taken seriously. Angst-packed, vision-limited, intoxicated by balmy nights and blossoms, they hold a moment so tightly it cracks like crystal. Love can come so early. You're pressured to misunderstand, to dismiss, to treat it as not quite real. Hey, Joe, would you believe something? I still miss you—like crazy!

Winter '51

The Nolan one-story box at 36 West 49th stands three lots east of the Taylor's larger stucco at 48, across from the football field and three houses west of the Nicollet streetcar line and St. John's Church—a Catholic fortress in Lutheran land. The streetcar stops at Nicollet and 49th and the ride north to downtown Minneapolis takes half an hour. The ride south to the end of the line at 54th takes only five minutes. Where the tracks end, houses and stores trail off until only acres of farmland and woods create a loamy wedge that fills the angle where the Minnesota River joins the Mississippi on its swirl to the slush of the Gulf.

Separated since before kindergarten by those three houses Joe and Kathy and Mickey grew up playing on the hills of Ramsey Junior and sometimes farther west on 49th at Washburn High. After a fall football game or spring track meet they'd search under the stands and collect pop bottles and ice cream wrappers to turn in at the grocers, sometimes finding coins or even a dollar bill. Summers when no one was around they'd take dares and scale the high, narrow ledges that frame the school walls. They'd roll on the endless grassy slopes, climb the fences, parade down the monumental steps, and build forts in cave-like shrubs. All that became theirs. And they never outgrew nor relinquished their ownership.

As sophomores, Kathy on crutches and Joe walk by the flat roof that extends west from Washburn's botany lab and greenhouse. Toward the corner of an L-shaped alley, a protective fence borders the hilltop near 49th that drops like a ski jump to the faculty parking lot. They stand in the alley behind the fence watching porch lights blink on as neighbors settle in for the evening. Melting snow bubbles down gutters to corner drains, and the fragrance of unlocking soil suggests the coming of forsythia.

Before ice turned to slush only the reckless pushed off this fence to belly flop on cardboard down the bumpy slide. Most spilled or chickened out partway down, rolling to the bottom hoping no car started suddenly in the lot. Joe says, "We used to be pretty dumb to go down that."

"Accidents happen every winter on this hill," Kathy says. "Cars crash into the concrete wall on 49th and I go get myself gimpy on a football fence."

"Come on," Joe says. Kathy, no longer in a cast, tosses her crutches aside and limps after him toward the flat roof.

She kicks to get a grip on the wall, her ripped loafer toe holding no penny. "Boost me up." Joe cups her foot, feeling layers of fabric under her ankle-length skirt, while she turns herself on the ledge.[12]

"Do you hurt?"

"Dragging my buns over bricks? Sure I hurt, but the damage's done."

They dangle their feet as though off a dock. "I have a hard time watching guys trying not to watch me walk."

"Think Tiny Tim and Long John Silver."

[12.] KN: What a wardrobe! Ankle length, for God's sake, when most skirts covered only the knees. At the FEMS Rummage Sale, held in a shabby space we rented near the action off Washington Avenue where the bums hover, I found more clothes to cover me than in stores. And I could pick them without a salesgirl telling me, "Oh, how nice that looks on you."

MN: Noble you! You had to wait two years before getting a learner's permit and you didn't complain much—except when the Boulevard Twins Theater put too little salt on your popcorn.

"Healthy folk like Eva Perõn and Ethel Rosenberg, huh?" She pats the wall next to her. "I may need you to defend me."

"Get Jud. He's got 50 pounds and mighty muscles I missed out on."

"Jud Albright may be second team All-City but he doesn't take time between seasons to shower." She reaches for the long window opening pole. Joe grabbed it from its hook to chase her from the *Grist* room where they were pasting galleys to make pages.

"If I defend you," Joe asks, "Will you lie for me to Lou Upson's Custodial Union? Will you testify, 'He took the pole for me'?"

"I'll swear you 'took pipe' *and* the 'Fifth Amendment.'"

"Evasions."

"Precisions! Bring the pole home so you'll be able to tap on my window."

"You want Romeo. Even though he can't bring his club back without breaking his wrists.

"Cole Porter already wrote about his Kate. Why don't we write our *Grist* musical about Ophelia—her boyfriend too, of course? If we can't find a singer we like better than Jeff Hatch, we can turn him upstage and make him saw air."

"Can we pull that off with homework and putting out a newspaper every two weeks?"

"Sure," Kathy says. "And do our college apps too. We'll be fine—if we don't go out weekends. My friends can locate the Boulevard Theater or Parkway without me. And I'm not exactly Washburn's dating queen."

"The Fab FEMS! God bless your little...."

"Careful."

"Back in 7th grade I was so in awe of you, Leggy, Cleo...."

"...and Amy too?"

"Amy too. You four had a special aura. You dressed so cool."

"*They* did. Look at me. Is this what dressing cool looks like? 'Little Ragged Red Kathy.' Mickey's dog wears a better coat."

"Let's write a show that will run forever," Joe says. "Start with a title. R & H named their first three for a state, a carnival ride, and a tempo: *Oklahoma! Carousel, Allegro.* We can name ours for Gertrude and Claude's favorite breakfast cereal at Elsinore, if you'll call General Mills and find out what they ate."

"A one-night run would be plenty good. A long run's what's under my skirt. I feel a runner racing down the stocking on my only remaining and oh-so-sexy leg. Or do runs run up? I know: you can't see up my skirt, and I'm not one of Carrie's skinny dippers."

"Let's base it on the 'Cask of Amontillado?' We'd need only one set. Or 'The Murders in the Rue Morgue.'"

"Bit of a casting problem," Kathy says. "Tell me: don't you ever feel like going ape? I'm not asking you to yearn for the outrageous? But have you ever even come close? I almost let myself go. Once! He turned out to be Minnesota's biggest button fumbler."

"How about a revue with sketches like Sid Caesar and Imogene?"

"Funnier, let's do Ike with Mamie, or Bess with Harry."

"You cold?"

"Crampy. Maybe we better clump back and paste the rest of the galleys?"

More house lights snap on. Plants darken under the greenhouse glass. "I'm sorry your stomach hurts."

"My stomach? Close guess, guy! A little girl's cramps generally come farther down. Tell me: if I stopped cutting dresses out of Amy's old sailcloth, would you pant over the cut of my jib?"

"You're doing all right, aren't you? So it happened. It doesn't show much. Just think: now you don't have to worry as much about getting something else bad, like polio. Your injury odds have dropped and your great life odds have skyrocketed."

"Up? Like Mickey's little pecker? I'm not exactly a sky-rocket girl."

"Look, you've won a lot of respect around school. Respect, not sympathy. Not counting *mucho* scowls from Mr. G."

"I'm okay, but I hope Mr. G. isn't. Does that sound like retaliation?"

"So he's a shit? When we get out in the world, he'll be stuck here."

"Maybe we can wrap his foot around the accelerator of that dumpy Nash; aim it up Pleasant, and watch him ram into the concrete wall."

"That *would* be retaliation. I think we did the right thing by *not* telling on him. Now he can never be sure when we might strike."

Kathy goes silent, then she's sobbing. Her head drops to his shoulder. His arm goes around her. He can feel where the bone below her elbow bends outward.

"I guess I *am* jealous," she says between sobs. "I'm jealous because I had to stand right next to you. There you were—going out of your gourd—trying to tell whether she was wearing anything. You could have asked for God's sake. No! Does it make you happy to know she wasn't wearing anything?"[13]

[13.] KN: I may have cried, but Joe could be so blind. We stood shoulder to shoulder by the bay that night—as a sophomore my head still higher than his—yet he didn't see me at all. And shit, I would have pulled my pants over my damn cast if he'd asked.

∽

JT: (Joseph "Joe" Taylor) Amy? This...this must be you.[14]

AJ: (Amy Johnson) This is she.

JT: Amy?

AJ: Yes.

JT: This is Joe Taylor. How ya doing?

AJ: Better than tomorrow.

JT: What?

AJ: Never mind.

JT: Tell you why I called. I called because I was wondering whether if, by any chance, you already had a date, or might want to go to the Formal, the Spring Formal. At the Calhoun Beach Club?

AJ: You want to know whether anyone's asked me? No. No one has.

JT: You mean you can go?

AJ: Yes.

JT: That's kind of great. And that's why I called. I guess we can talk about more, later. Maybe tomorrow in homeroom.

AJ: The Formal's not for two months. By then you should be able to find me. Ask Mr. Hallam. He'll show you my stool up front by the window.

JT: I know. I've seen you sitting on it.

AJ: And yours is way back! You might have trouble finding my house. It's got snow all over it. But in two months that might melt. I live in Tangletown—down the hill from Page Elementary.

JT: I know: the school where the FEMS went. You don't even have to ask for permission to go out, huh? That's great.

AJ: That's been great since 8ᵗʰ grade. I don't suppose you can drive?

---

14.   KN: Why should I act surprised. I saw this call coming before he dreamed it.

JT: Dad said he'd drive us. Oh, and Happy Birthday! Kathy said you had a birthday. You must be fifteen too.

AJ: I might have been on Wednesday, but we didn't have February 29 this year. Mom's teaching me to drive the green Chevy. Ours only holds daddy's car, so we rent a garage down the alley across 51st.

JT: I've only been fifteen since June, so we'll be the same age for four months. I get my permit this summer.

AJ: Who's going to teach you? Kathy?

JT: She just seems older. Look, maybe I'll see ya round your locker before homeroom. We don't have to decide everything right away. We have plenty of time for everything.

Spring '51[15]

In his rented tux Joe knocks on the Johnson door while his father waits in the Taylor car at the curb. Late spring flakes fall on Joe's perspiring neck and fresh crew cut.

When the door swings open a man stands with his folded newspaper, peering out as though Joe might be collecting for the *Tribune*. "You must be the one for Amy." He calls up the stairs, "There's another someone here, unless you're not expecting someone." He faces Joe. "I assume she's the one you want. Only daughter I've got, far as I know."

---

15. MN: Hey, Babe, didn't we blow one? Aren't you supposed to dedicate one of these beauties?

KN: The book? Okay. Make it simple. "To HH." That's not, by the way, Humphrey or Hoover, Helen Hunt Jackson, Helen Hunt the Cheerleader Quarterback, Humbert Humbert, Saki, or Hoscar Hammerstein II. 'Tis Helena Hermia.

MN: Reverse that and you'll still have a beast with two backs.

KN: Don't knock any relationship. In those woods by Athens those pretty girls will never pause for thee: they were sweet flowers who sported elbows you'd die for, lab partners ideal for the chem class you never took.

MN: Not die! And I never had a lav partner. Could I take one on our kitchen table with flour all over it like Nicolson takes Jessica in the remake of *The Postman Rings Twice*?

KN: Crude! And typical. I know we're supposed to become more accepting of our sexuality, but your mouth reminds me of a sweaty pit.

MN: Okey dokey. I'll pick up a fresh set of whites.

KN: Yes, do wear something under your shorts. Small stuff to sweat maybe, but....

MN: Hey! Don't get personal! Remember: this is only a book.

Joe manages, "You're a doctor I understand."

"If you understand you must be one too. No, tonight I'm a patient. A patient reading box scores and obituaries."

"I guess you do surgery?"

"During my rotation! I don't volunteer."

"What about emergencies?"

"I prefer roses. Do you grow roses?"

Thick medical sets fill three walls of the study left of the stairs. A grand piano fills a corner of the living room to the right. The doctor offers Joe a seat on the sofa facing the stairs. He sits, trying to picture all that Amy must do up there to get dressed. "I guess I didn't know Amy played. Or is it you or Mrs. Johnson?"

"Oh, it's my talented tot. She sails her D-Class on Calhoun and plays her major chords right here. Her buoy's below the Minikahda Club. Nice fellows. Fine gardens."

"My grandfather, my first one—I had three on my mother's side *and* three on my father's—used to grow roses."

"Is the good gardener still with us?"

"He had gardens on the North Shore of Chicago, pretty huge ones. I don't think he did much of the gardening himself."

"You don't do surgery by yourself anymore. I never know who's under all the masks they crowd into my theater. Might be Dave Garroway or Howdy Doody. You watch them?"

"Not too often."

"With roses I do it all myself."

"I've got roses here." Joe holds up a box. "I imagine you need lots of patience to grow them."

"Too many patients. Does anyone on your father's side grow roses?"

"Dad's an accountant. Works late a lot—nights."

"Gardening's harder in the dark. Otherwise I'd operate less and plant more. Sunlight on your hatband: that's a true feeling! Or don't you wear a hat?"

"I usually wear a visor—for golf."

"Golf? Is that a team sport? The boys who stop here don't wear hats except when it's baseball season or below zero. If you want to read their names on the log, you'll have to ask Mrs. Johnson, Marie—she's my charming wife. I don't keep count. I do enjoy reading about them though. Can I get you a drink?"

"No, Sir. No, thank you."

"Did I sound serious? Mrs. Johnson says people find it hard to tell. I don't keep much hard stuff here. Patients prefer their doctors—probably their dentist and barber—to have fresh breath as well as steady hands. I bet you brushed your teeth twice. They look fine. Peppermint? I suppose barbers have it best; they never get night calls. Peanut?"

"No, thank you, Sir."

"Good. Don't keep any of those around either. Salt's a killer. That's what the Internal Medicine boys want us to believe. Marie! Come meet the new one. I'm betting we see him a second time. He called me, 'Sir.'"

"Sorry. I should have said, 'Dr.'"

"You did fine. Here in my castle near the creek I answer to 'Sir'—even to 'Lord.' Save 'Doctor' till you're trying to reserve my table at the hospital. I discount all of Amy's friends—even former friends who used to stop by."

"Thank you, Dr. I mean, Sir."

"Don't thank me. I don't accept her invitations. She keeps her own records. But I keep her away from my opera records. I found a scratch on Carmen right after she's convinced Don José to race off to the hills. My new needle won't ride through it."

"We usher at the Lyceum when musical shows come through. We don't get operas, but I love musicals," Joe says. "We're getting both Oklahoma! and Allegro this spring."

"'Love?' Have you composed much on that concept? When the weather warms, sit under an elm and contemplate that—profoundly. That nice young fellow—name like 'Meal' or 'Seal'—always said he loved basketball. He was a tall drink, always hugging his pimply basketball. Actually his own skin was clearer than most your age. He scored a lot of points—assists too. Good things: assists. You agree? I love opera, roses, and my daughter—and of…." Joe stands as Mrs. Johnson enters the room. "…of course you too, my dear."

The doctor sits and opens his paper, like Joe, glancing toward the stairs.

"Joseph! How nice to see you again." Mrs. Johnson gestures so Joe sits back on the sofa.

The doctor says, "You didn't tell me the boy already made rounds here."

"Joe's in Amy's homeroom. His father works with me on PTA budgets. Joe's quite active too."

"This year we've started to get a ton of homework."

"Marie, does Amy bring home anything like that?"

"Big difference since we started high school."[16]

"That visor? Do you swing a fancy set of clubs under it? I thought young fellows saw golf as an old folks game?"

"Not with a Hogan or Snead. I play Spaulding woods with Hagen irons. You can play golf all your life."

"Then it *must* be worthwhile. I'll take you to the Country Club if you're still dropping by when the snow melts. Never could get that Seal guy to put down his basketball long enough to join me."

"It was Neal, dear."

"Neal Hastings," Joe says. "All-city forward three years ahead of us. A senior when we were finishing Ramsey. Most points in a single season—a record breaker."

"Would you call *Carmen* a record breaker? I never could get that boy to listen to my opera records. I would have awarded him an assist for that. Did he like musical shows, Marie?"

[16.] KN: Remember 10th grade geometry? Everyone said, "Wait for Mr. Hunter." Picture him planting one elbow on the chalkboard and swinging his arm in a perfect circle, unbroken, like a dancer pointing forward with each spin. Afterwards Mr. Hunter'd look up with a straight face as though he hadn't done a thing.
MN: What did he do? I didn't take geometry. Or any maths.
KN: Or any academics!

"Don't make Joe uncomfortable, dear." Steps tap on a floorboard above, then go silent. "I believe Neal came around so often because he enjoyed talking to the doctor."

"I doubt that." Dr. Johnson looks over his paper.

"And he *was* a bit of a hypochondriac," Mrs. Johnson says. "Neal kept visiting here long after he stopped taking Amy out."

"They went out most of last year. *Our* 9th grade," Joe says.

"How about 'Twice Across'?" Dr. Johnson asks. "As a sportsman you *must* play cribbage? If we're up when you get back from this—whatever it is?"

"Formal, dear. The Spring Formal at the Calhoun Beach Club."

"Way out there? Across from Minikahda? All those stuffy members?"

"I've caddied there," Joe says. "If you're lucky, your loop will buy you a soda between nines. If you go 36 carrying double, you can earn $10 if each player tips you a quarter."

"I wouldn't fail to offer a cold soda when someone comes out of anesthesia if it were medically wise. Wouldn't cost me much; I could bill the hospital—or the patient. If our lights are on when you come home, Warner, we'll play a few cribs."

"Please don't tease. His name is not Warner. This is Joe Taylor, Junior."

"Junior now, but I'm sure he'll grow up and have to play in the Senior League some day. Excuse me, I have to finish the evening *Tribune* before the boy buries the morning *Star* in a snowdrift. Marie, it's your turn to keep the conversation peppy. You're right: this *is* a nice boy and 'Warner' is too formal—even for a Formal. We'll call him 'Joe.'"

Steps approach on the landing. Into Joe's range move yellow pumps, clear meshed calves, whirling crinoline, and daffodil taffeta. He's never seen her in stockings and heels, or noticed the narrowness of her waist pinched between rises of daffodil. She has darkened the dot next to her mouth, crowned her lemon hair with a headache band, and dangled golden seashells from her ears.

She totters as she starts down, reaching for the banister, but holding her crown high and level. The hose over one ankle wrinkles as she steps closer. She nods: a booming tinkle announcing her entrance. Stairs creak and taffeta rustles. From his corner the doctor examines his loveliest rose.

Joe hands her the box. "Here are some flowers."

"How nice," her mother says. "Would you like to wear my coat? My boots?"

"I'll be fine with my camel's hair." Amy's voice hovers with the same flatness she produces from her stool in homeroom. Joe remembers Hatch shouting from the boys' side of the cafeteria so the girls across the aisle could hear, "Hell's bells, she's built like a boy!"

Joe hears Kathy calling, "She's not exactly the best-read, most ambitious of our friends."[17]

Under snowflakes Joe doesn't feel confident enough to offer an arm, but he stays close. He knows any serious talking must happen before they reach the car because his father is driving. She wobbles again on her high heels, but doesn't reach for him.

"Do those really keep your legs warm?"

"My nylons? They cut down the wind, but I'm not going to drop on a drift and move my arms and legs to make an angel."

"Who's Warner?"

"Warner?"

"Your father kept calling me Warner."

"Oh, for heaven's sake! That's my bra brand. He's impossible. Ever since I wore a Single A, 32, and each time I've changed—not often, in case you didn't notice—he's given me

---

[17.] KN: That makes me sound like a snippy shit. Amy never pretended to try for better than "B's" and I think she got those. She didn't practice enough basketball to sweat.

MN: So?

KN: When Joe felt infatuated I wanted him to learn more about possibilities in the world. I figured there would always be plenty of girls who would jump at the chance to share their lives with him. I always knew I would. My mother told me. So did all my body's warmest places.

a hard time. And he's the adult! I think when you go to a doctor you deserve a Saint, complete with an arrow in the side so both hands will be free to work. Don't let daddy get to you. Don't picture him holding a scalpel, reading an X-ray, and looking right through you."

"Can *you* do that?"

"Sure! I can tell that you're going to try to hold my hand, maybe kiss me and ask me out again."

"Will you?"

"What?"

"Go out with—me. Maybe next Friday?"

"Can't!"

"Saturday?"

"Nope!"

"I'm not asking to hold your hand or kiss you. Just a movie?"

"Are you any fun? For heaven's sake, you're only one of 500 in our class—one of 30 in our homeroom. Why should I go out with you twice—even though we do have over a hundred weekends before graduation? If you need to know, Jeff already asked me out for next Friday."[18]

Joe holds the car door. She slides across the backseat to sit politely behind Joe's father who will drive them to the Formal and drive them home when it's over.

---

18. KN: She was a perfectly nice girl, Joe, unusually clean and only unconsciously a tease.

   MN: But I was waiting to watch Joe rock in a hammock with Carrie Browne. If he'd gotten to her before she moved north, he could have combed her brown arm hairs rather than swinging Johnson's ponytail. That's not to say I wouldn't have wrinkled my corduroys in the backseat with Amy, whether or not she carried a rubber in her purse. And no one—girl *or* boy—carried rubbers back then. A nice girl'd probably never seen one—even in a picture.

   KN: And you didn't see phosphorated hesperidin in a friend's medicine cabinet.

   MN: Come again!

   KN: Birth control pills!

↜

During one of the few masses Kathy manages to drag him to, Mickey feels a pulsing to match the pipes in the organ when he watches Frankie Hill and her kid sister kneel. He seldom gets this close to either.[19]

Across the aisle Frankie, young at fourteen, crosses herself. So does her even younger sister—both jailbait. They glow more than the altar's polished candlesticks. Frankie looks better than bibles, but Mickey knows if he lets the large charge she gives him propel him across the aisle she'll grab her sister and run for the sanctuary.

Frankie's in the class behind his, where she's twice turned the heads of every 9th grade boy—plus college men, teachers, mailmen, male guppies, anyone who pumps blood into what Kathy calls, "A boy's little thing-ee."

Frankie and her sister kneel on four glorious knees, two covered by pink cotton and two meshed by clear silk. Her sister tugs at her veil and Frankie lets the back of one heel come out of her shiny pumps. Mickey wonders whether she ever needs help polishing them.[20]

At the close of mass Mickey keeps kneeling, folding his face in his hands, fingers open, to watch the sisters pass. At the door, Frankie looks back and smiles. Perhaps at him.[21]

[19.] MN: What can I say?

KN: Tell the truth. You must remember that.

MN: I just did!

[20.] MN: Come off it, Kath, you make me sound like a puppy panting. If I was that obvious the priest would have plopped me in the baptismal font and sat on the lid. Sure Frankie Hill was a looker, but she wasn't about to give me any time.

KN: Frankie defined gorgeous and athletic, but the poor thing always had to worry about a sudden attack. *Grand mal.*

MN: Epilepsy! I saw her roll down the Ramsey steps, jerking and thrashing until Carrie pushed a ruler between her teeth.

KN: A second Florence Nightingale, our pseudo-ersatz Southern "Lady Belle Carrie."

MN: Frankie was 4' 10" and 95 pounds, all cuddle poured into a leotard and tights. But on the beam or bar her eyes always looked scared that she might suddenly spasm in front of the whole school.

[21.] MN: Hot damn!

Amy smiles as Moira Shearer's red shoes carry her closer
to the oncoming train. "I like it, I like it," Amy squeals in her
Jerry Lewis voice. "Best movie ever—about trains."

"Why would she do that?" Joe asks. "She heard the train
coming toward her."

"You have to be a woman to understand. It was the red
shoes. Will you buy me some? Pink if you'll feel safer."

They walk to her mother's car, parked in the Dinkytown
area of the University by the Varsity Theater. She gives him
a kiss and a key ring. "I had this set made. If you're good
you can keep it. One for the Chevy, one for the shed, two for
the garages. I'm not trusting you with a house key—yet."

"What's the fifth one do?"

"You know those belts women get locked into before their
men ride off to battle or golf?"

"You're kidding me?"

As they drive he feels her head on his lap below the steering wheel. He holds her steady and drives carefully. Under
her vanilla camel's hair coat her skirt rides above her shiny
knees. He strokes the cushion of hair resting on his lap as
they pass the State Fairgrounds.

He turns down a boulevard of buds. "I didn't plan it," he
says. "But I think we're in Como Park. The zoo! Only us!
Smell it."

"The animals?"

"The trees! Everything about to bud and blossom."

"A zoo at night with blossoms—and melting snow. What
would our parents say? They always worry when we get in
late. Always worry we've done something we're not supposed to."

"Same as the church, Y-clubs, Scouts. They want to make
us scared to death of—you know...."

"Someone getting 'preggers'—like mainly *moi*?"

"Yeah, my parents worried about that before I knew how it even happened."

"I've got bears and giraffes to protect me." Her nose tip bumps the steering wheel. "I haven't been here since I rode a stroller down the wide walk by the cages and concession stands. Try for red shoes. If you can't come up with 'em, buy me a red balloon."

They coast down the slope to the arched pavilion, where paddleboats will soon dot the lake. He follows the road that curves away from the lake and climbs past rocky ledges to shadows below a bluff.

"I guess we're here," Joe says. "Do you suppose we can rent a cage for Mickey?"

"'Nolan' or 'Mouse'? Turn off the engine. Daddy checks the gauge."[22]

"We can buy gas."

"Not before I get my shoes or balloon. Come on, let's catch an animal." She leans across to open the door, rolling over him, heels tapping as she crosses the parking lot to the bluff.

She points and climbs under the darkness of boulders blocking the moon. He follows past dark caves for the bears, hesitating below the steep stair. "I hear something."

"Boa constrictor about to slap your leg. Take one giant step forward." He jumps and reaches for her. "Don't touch. Daddy checks me for fingerprints—he's a doctor. You're not, so you can't check me." She knocks Joe into what's left of a snowdrift and keeps tapping fast in her navy heels.

[22.] MN: Dad always said you could count on a good Standard Station or a diner where rows of truckers parked.

KN: The washrooms dad stopped at had water and wet towels on the floor and broken locks.

MN: Don't knock Dad! But I seriously doubt that Dr. Johnson walked down the alley and crossed 51st to check the gas gauge on Mrs. Johnson's Chevy.

KN: That walk from the rented garage back to Amy's house worried Joe. He wouldn't let her drop him off at his house but insisted on walking her up the alley, so then he had to hike home all the up the 50th street hill. These days that would make a lot of sense!

MN: Then it was dumb.

He calls, "What if cops come by?"

"I'm up here. You fix it with them. The zoo's public."

"They'll trace the plates to your house."

"Not to a rented garage. Mom won't give us away. Not if I were to imply that you and I...feel...oh, some attraction. Mom has the hots for all my boyfriends. Daddy reserves judgment, but you've got a good start." Her shadow blends with other shadows.

She calls down, "Smell the caramel apples? Gotta find them. Bees won't start landing until the sun comes up."

Suddenly she's back, clicking past him down the steps. She crosses the parking lot and scrambles in the passenger door. "Best zoo ever!"

"Better than the Bronx?"

"And Staten Island too! But it's too dark. Find us a paradise where moon dances, or lop off the bluff top so we can see the lake. You look like a ghost in the dark. Like nothing. I can't even tell whether you're dressed."

He eases the Chevy around the caves, rising and circling until they drop again above the lake. "Well, here we are." He's self-conscious going through the teen parking ritual: coughing, key turn, brake-pull, pause. Suddenly her Moira Shearer smile and mad-under-the-moon face have fallen away. She sits against her door, flat-eyed as in study hall. "What's the matter?"

"Why did you stop?" A branch swings shadows across the windshield. A silence extends itself. He reaches to touch her and as suddenly as she changed from her smile she changes to it, sliding close so their arms lock around each other.

"Why do you make it so hard sometimes?"

"I've never done this. Alone in the zoo? Me alone with you?"

"Whenever you sit way over against the door I feel stupid. What if someone broke the window and reached in?"

She pushes a limp wrist in his face, making her "Pheer!" sound to suggest his dumbness.

He takes her wrist. She shakes off his hand so she can slide out of her coat and drop it on the backseat. He says, "Maybe you'll...do...lots of this. I mean with other people, maybe."

Her limp wrist thrusts at him again. "Pheer! What do you want me to say? Possibly? Lots? Never? What about what you might do?"

"Someday you mean?" He runs a finger over her scar.

"Do you want me to think about other people someday?"

"Why would I want that?" he asks.

"I don't want you to want me to. It's just that...Oh, why can't we just...*be* here?"

"I guess we are." He buries his face in her neck, blowing until her earrings flutter. "Hello."

"Hello," she purrs. "You're not worried now?"

"I'm happy. Happier than...."

Her arms tighten, an elbow bumping the dashboard. Her heels brace against the heater. She stops to wipe off her lipstick with a Kleenex.

He wets a finger to pick a wisp from her lip, replacing it with his mouth. "You smell so good. Like a store."

"So do you, but not like a store."

"What's the neat scent?"

She drawls, "T-a-b-u. Eau de toilette. It comes in a very small bottle—from the drug store, not Dayton's.'"

"I like it. And you, and our zoo."

"I'll wear it whenever we're here. My zoo perfume—it's really cologne."

"I like everything about you."

"Golly! I bet you're only saying that because I'm a girl." Her hand touches his face, fingers stroking. He wraps her fingers in a bunch, prying away her handkerchief. He trails it across her mouth, then lets it smooth the outside of her cashmere front, pressing lightly.

"Your handkerchief's sort of like purple."

"Have you heard of lavender?"

"And it's folded."

"I never unfold them."

"What's it for then?"

"For my purse. Using it's taboo too, but I'll let you borrow it if you have your library card."

He teases her nose with it. "Is this how they put you to sleep?"

"Doctors? Like when they did this?"

He touches her throat, then drops both hands to circle her waist, hugging, before returning to the shoulders of her sweater.

"There are other parts of me beside my scar and mole. Like other girls. Big surprise, I bet. But I'm not sure they're for you. I already let you borrow my handkerchief. We'll have to see."

Joe tucks her handkerchief in his shirt pocket. He feels it, and more, between them when they press together. "You know that Easter card you sent me? The drawing of two bears on a ledge: one saying, 'Let's fall for each other; you first!'"[23]

Holding tight, she smiles up at him. He whispers, "Well, I *have*!"

Amy keeps looking at him, lips partly open.

"If you sent that card and we can be like this…. Why would we ever want to go out with anyone else? You did, a year ago, after the dance."

"Once! I'd already promised."

"Everytime we go out, and we've gone out every Friday and Saturday for a year, not counting all the time in the hallways…."

"I've been along, haven't you noticed?"

"Well everytime we go out I don't like having to ask."

"Have I ever said, 'No'?"

"No."

[23.] MN: A Hallmark cheapy?

KN: Stop that! They're serious. Amy had taste. You have to remember how sweet and sad this seems, knowing what we know about how it all came out.

"Then don't sweat it, sweetie. Don't make trouble before it comes."

"I've never really wanted to 'go steady.' I'd rather not have people use that word about us."

"We wouldn't have to call it 'going steady.' I don't want a fat ring wound with dirty tape. We could simply have... 'an understanding.' *Our* understanding!"

"And we can still go out all the time?"

"If you want us to."

"Let's do that. It'll be 'our private understanding.' Unless like in *Oklahoma!* I get a hankering to shout out that you're my girl so, 'Let people say we're in love.'"

"You want me to say that, don't you?"

"You almost did."

"I have trouble saying things that I can write down."

"Like the card with the two bears?"

"I *bought* that."

"You chose it and signed it."

He slides his hands down the wool over her ribs to where she narrows before widening. Sliding back up he wonders whether he's only holding her sides or might actually be touching the outer edges of her modest fullness.

She does not move until headlights splash, forcing them to duck. Joe snaps the locks, just in case.

The glare passes, leaving them alone on the budding land above the lake.

"So we've made an understanding?" he says.

"We've created a quiet, wonderful understanding, which can last as long as...."

"Forever!" He hears himself rushing to say. "You gave me your Tabu handkerchief. It's from the drug store; it's lavender; it's you folded into my hand."

"...for—as long as you like."

"For forever and...."

⌒

MN: Well, Kate, my gal. Dids't or didns't he? I'm talking our boy Joe, the Little Princess, and kissy-face fun at the zoo.

KN: The night balm of thawing April snow: I'll wager one kiss. Their first! Not a mite more.

MN: No, I think by Zoo Night they were already playing like magnets.

KN: Enough so you could read about them in *Confidential?*

MN: Enough like the wine of a fine mass, unless one of their noses dripped from a nasty cold into the chalice.

KN: Give me a moment to put on my pith helmet. There: have I placed it as jauntily as the good Colonel Schweppes?

MN: Actually I think they roared right out of the box, heavy after the Spring Formal.

KN: Except that one Friday interruption from dubiously respected Class President Hatch. Yes, in the halls they did demonstrate that surfeiting inseparability that some classmates accepted, but I found a bit much. You remember how they whispered about Leggy and Jeff in 9th grade when they'd be spotted emerging from a backseat. I like and respect Leggy, but....

MN: But no one could confirm whether or not they were doing the nasty, *correctomounto?*

KN: Pretty soon teachers needed chisels to separate Joe and Amy into the right classrooms. They went out every weekend night except that first Friday after the Formal when she went out with Jeff.

MN: Once? You sure?

KN: Pretty sure.

MN: Tut, twit! You had your admirers too. Why I believe Mr. G. had a scooner for you. And with your gentle nature, I know you have a mature tolerance for—what should we call them—perhaps "dirty old men" says it all. But I'm sure, if given the opportunity, you'd employ precautionary prophylactics.

KN: Precautionary prophylactics? A redundancy, fella. Anyway no offers. Maybe we *should* have ganged up more on Washburn's Gestapo Chief.

MN: Too late now. Him tucked into Lakewood across the slopes from Hubert Humphrey's tasteful corner graveyard wall. But back to our boy Joe: dids't or didns't he?

KN: Their breath frosted the Chevy windows so we can't be sure of positions. But we know when she drove her mother's car he felt diminished.

MN: I bet she let him drive, putting her on the passenger side. At least to start. Maybe he didn't make the first move. Maybe he didn't do it. End of discussion.

KN: You said they roared right out of the box. Besides, he told me he did.

MN: Did? Did he say they made "kissy-face"?

KN: They sipped love's bubbles.

MN: Oh, please! No sipping—or sucking—at that stage.

KN: The big parental warning—stated more formally: "Keep your thing from getting too close to hers."

MN: And versa visa.

KN: And without AIDS to scare the shit out of them they could focus on the great hickey epidemic. Or plain old pimples.

MN: Amy was a clean little thing. Delicate skin, the fragrance of....

KN: Chesterfields! Leggy told me how at age 13 they'd sneak away from Happy Hollow at Camp Lake Hubert. And one night: a few puffs on a Tiparillo! But Amy never became a high school smoker like Cleo, so she figured Joe didn't need to know.

MN: Details about camp life? Miss Cleo you say?

KN: She smoked like a campfire and always left a hairy razor in the shower. The time Joe saw butts in the Chevy's ashtray Amy passed them off as Cleo's. And they might have been.

MN: King Gillette ground out a wicked blue blade in those days: a double-edged job for slicing balsa wood and our fingers when we made Spitfires and Stukas because we couldn't afford an X-Acto set. So what cute little swimsuit would Mother Johnson have packed for Miss Amy?

KN: Wouldn't matter. She'd buy her own when the bus stopped in Brainerd. Probably a bikini—like the girls in Dayton's Skyroom modeled to the accompaniment of Dick Long's orchestra.

MN: The bikini! Nice eye, cow pie! Hard to believe that hasn't always been with us. And yes, I know, not as tasty as hair pie, but a bikini leaves the breast—I mean best covered.

KN: Hubert was an all-girls camp. Except for those wonderful handymen who lurked when the campers snuck off to skinny dip in Bass Lake. Amy's first kiss did not come in Como Park Zoo.

MN: Well, how 'bout her 81st and 82nd kiss? Maybe it was her 83rd when he said goodnight at her door on Zoo Night.

KN: He does and she does. And little jazz birds do.

MN: Did he mention climaxes or a bit of dry humping?

KN: Endings! Always endings, and too damn soon.

MN: An orgiastric lasts longer than a sneeze. Though boys don't get them one after another like sneezes.

KN: Is "orgasm" the word you're chasing. Or are you trying for "orgiastic?" That's how *Gatsby* ends.

MN: Before you said he got shot by that garage guy.

KN: That's different.

MN: Orgastic sounds plenty dirty to me.

KN: Grow up. You're looking back. They were only fifteen when this happened?

MN: When what happened? When fresh fifteen Amy built Joe another hard-on while pressing a heel into her papa's front door?

KN: "Hard-on" sounds vulgar.

MN: Well, you don't get one to disappear by wishing. Pinocchio couldn't. Of course he got his from telling lies.

KN: Joe doesn't tell lies.

MN: How about Amy? What she told Joe about Hatch?

KN: She told him the truth about that one time.

MN: So what about the Raleigh guy from Southwest? She went out with him Easter Sunday.

KN: I guess I did hear that.

MN: Has she told Joe? Will she?

KN: I don't know.

MN: He never did anything like that. Not until *much* later.

Spring '52

Amy tunes fuzz from an oval Philco screen, the only light in her basement. She says her parents will never bother them there. She's barefoot below pink pedal pushers and her father's white shirt. She bends forward to tie the tails together, showing straps inside the unbuttoned collar.

Joe says, "I think about how you look too much."

"Can't do that."

She stands over him, arms at her sides like a diver. Then she falls forward, suspending herself with a hand on each side of Joe's waist before curling into his lap, tucking under her faintly bristled calves.

"Ticklish?" he asks while memorizing the spacing between each rib.

"No. But *you* are." She digs with her thumbs until he has to hold her off, pushing so the too-large shirt slides loosely over her. Her shirt feels dry and stiff with starch and he hopes she doesn't notice that his is wet beneath the arms.

She yawns, adjusts her position and a shoulder strap, straddling him with knees and fists. Her shirt rides up so he sees a rough ridge: a not new scar the span of his fingers.

"That's one daddy *did* do. He goofed the other time."

They hold hands and lean back like rowers resting on an oar. "Stitches?"

"Pheer!" She pushes a limp wrist at him. "They generally need stitches to close a hole."

He runs his fingers across the scar. "Your appendix? Here?"

"They're in a jar now." She pokes his belly. "Routine for a doctor's daughter. I had the worst cramps ever. Didn't want to move. Wouldn't have made it if a doctor wasn't already scrubbing and a nurse gloved to prep me."

"Prep?"

"That's a little lather and a dull razor. It itched awful as it grew back. Thicker, but not enough to cover the scar. Nobody can see unless I pull my pedal pushers down when I'm not wearing panties, which I'm not going to do. Would you like me if I did that?"

"You're here and...I think...I think I love you." He tastes her tongue. Her hands tangle his hair. But she doesn't say what he wants to hear.

"Now! You've heard about my secret scar!"

"How about the scar on your throat?"

"My trach mark? Number two in my Wonderful World of Scars? I went to bed with a stuffy nose. Pretty soon I couldn't breathe. I went in their room—mommy and daddy always sleep in the same bed. Daddy said it could wait. Mommy called another doctor. Daddy was wrong. You're supposed to cut with a piece of glass, coat hanger, anything to open the breathing passage. I came out of that okay, too. That's how I got my trach mark. Trach's for tracheotomy. I'm twice wounded but only one shows—as long as I stay dressed."

"How old were you?"

"Old enough to be careful about gowns with slits. I'm not like Leggy. In gym she pulls her shorts and underwear off and marches right through the footbath into the steam. Doesn't bother with those napkin-size towels until she comes out. Cleo doesn't much care who sees what either. And she's got a poor self-image—that's why she smokes."

"So how old were you?"

"I could still get into the movies for twelve cents and it was before streptomycin, so 6th grade. But I was maturing. The period part began before I was in the hospital. I started turning as early as anyone. By 6th grade I was probably plenty fertile."

"The tops of your legs: they're so round."

"All women are big there."

"Why?"

"Duh! I'll tell you someday—when you need to know. It's about having babies."

She stands so the television sparkles through, showing the lines of her underwear. He pictures corn tassels turned dark. "I don't like the idea of anyone seeing you, even your father."

"Daddy doesn't look closely at anything unless it's on his table or in his garden. But for girls, going to a doctor is not too neat. They make you sit like this for the worst part." She pushes her feet against him, plopping her heels on the cushions. "They make you push your feet into steel stirrups. You shiver so they cover you with a sheet. Then the doctor folds it back and there you are: all open underneath. Then with a nurse standing guard, he pokes inside, talking as though you don't know where his hands are. Be glad you're a boy and don't have to face a speculum. Actually you don't face it— worse than that. They call all that 'a pelvic'. Or do they do things to boys I haven't heard about?"

"Nothing like that. They prick us for blood."

"If you want to learn more we can look in the den. Daddy's medical books show everything. But you need a special library card for the volume with the ob-gyn pictures or his autographed Norman Vincent Peale."

He touches her throat. But when he reaches her beauty mark she grabs his hand. "Stay away!"

"Are you afraid it will rub off?"

"It doesn't rub off. It's real."

"Why's it smudged?"

"I twirl a pencil over it. I have a real mole—sort of smallish."

"I hate your father for…. For almost blowing it when you couldn't breathe."

"I thought you liked him. I do. He's the Albert Schweitzer of 5106 Luverne. Don't forget, you might make a mistake someday."

He lifts her lightness, lavender floating with a hint of orange soda. "We're locked," he says. "Does my belt buckle hurt?"

"Does mine?"

"You're not wearing a belt."

"I might be wearing a contour corset, or a belt you can't see."

"Without stockings?"

"Dummy, you don't need stockings to wear a belt. I can wear as much or as little as I want. How do you know I'm not wearing a belt like a good girl to protect my…you know …like knights and maidens?"

"You've never even seen one of those. They don't mount them in museums like armor."

"Well I haven't been fitted for new skates either. I'll show you my closet sometime. All the shoes lined up by heel height. In my dresser the nylons and cottons are lined up by color. You've seen my gold headache band, but next to it I keep my Wonder Woman magic wristbands. Smack! Thwack! Better watch it, fella."

"If you *did* wear…one of those things, would you really give me the key? You did joke about the fifth key on the set you gave me"

"Depends."

"On what?"

"On how I felt. Maybe I'm too small now."

Joe turns off "Our Miss Brooks." The only light now comes from under the door at the top of the stairs. "Look, Amy, I have to ask you something."

"Did you turn off the television so my parents can hear us better?"

SPRING '52 • 49

"This is serious. It's about our understanding. Kathy said that someone said they saw you at the movies with Jim Raleigh. The guy from Southwest."

"So?"

"We're not supposed to go out with anyone else."

"One movie. Not even a double-feature."

"Hatch, then Raleigh.That's two."

"Jeff came before the zoo."

"Another thing. I'd like to add something to our understanding."

"A small ring?"

"Not a ring. Look, I've never seen you smoke. I couldn't stand that. Those cigarettes in the ashtray that you said were Cleo's? Well, can we say as part of the understanding that you'll never smoke?"

"If I liked to, I would. But you don't have to worry, I don't. And I'm sorry. I suppose I should have turned Jim down when he asked me. Okay?"

"I would never do anything you didn't want," he says.

"I wouldn't let you do anything I didn't want."

They start one of their nonending kisses and hold tight to each other until one of her parents raps on the basement door.[24]

---

[24] KN: The scene heats up. Those two had a lot of hands moving. I wonder how far they *had* gone by "Tell me about your operation night."

MN: She wasn't stacked but, "More than a handful's a waste." Who would know that better than you, Miss Big Ones? Why did he have such a hang up about Amy smoking?

KN: A psychology course would have you introduced to phallic symbols. Picture a penis.

MN: Now you *are* putting me on. Think of something hard.

⌒

The Sunday after Jeff takes Amy out again, Joe joins the boys going cruisin'. At a garage and package store by Lake Minnetonka they run into two local girls. The decent-looking one climbs in front between Jeff and Luther. They ask her name and she says she's Gerta Stalacta. The other says she's Loraine Herring and sits in back with Mickey and Joe.

Driving faster than before, Jeff says, "Of course we can buy beer! You saw us back there."

"You were buying gas," Gerta says. "You guys rich?"

Loraine asks, "What grade ya in?"

"We're sophomores at the U," Mickey says.

The girls direct Jeff to a shack in the woods way beyond the jazz joints at Spring Lake Park. A guy materializes to sell them a six-pack for $5 a bottle. Mickey pays with the gas money that everyone has anteed in on the dashboard except him.

Jeff steers with the Necker Knob and tips his bottle without drinking. Joe also tries not to swallow, but fizz falls over his chin. Jeff circles St. Alban's Bay before pulling into the empty lot of the Old Log Theater, where he puts an arm around Gerta.

Mickey's hand roves over and under Loraine's bra, eventually managing to unhook it. Loraine doesn't seem to pay attention, making Joe feel even more awkward with his hip touching a girl while she's being felt up.

Gerta seems to get a charge out of winging back lines like, "Zap, I'm pregnant!" She makes a voice like a cop and orders Mickey, "Okay fella, lick your finger!"

Loraine takes the bottle Jeff's obviously not drinking, while keeping an eye on Joe and his bottle. Jeff starts the engine and pulls out of the lot. He heads them toward Highway 100, the Belt Line that circles the Twin Cities.

Loraine leans across Joe's lap and tosses the bottle into the other lane. It splinters—and echoes.

Jeff accelerates so they can ditch the girls back at the garage.

Joe wishes he hadn't come along, but knows he has to get Jeff alone to say something about his going out with Amy.

Mr. Miller teaches Joe's favorite class: Junior English.[25] It's the only class Joe takes with Amy. Miller's the only teacher who will call teacher Mrs. Mullins "an old bitch" and Mr. G. "a Nazi"—same as the students do. Carrie Browne feels sorry for Mr. Miller. "The poor guy wears those shirts with frayed collars and lives next to the railroad tracks." Joe knows Mr. Miller lives away from the palatial houses in the Kenwood neighborhood that borders the bays of Lake of the Isles.

But Old Willie Miller gets even kids who only keep seats warm asking questions about kings and queens, not the gentry of Minneapolis' suburbs and Minnetonka's wealthy lake sprawl, but real royalty. On the blackboard he chalks the route the new Queen will walk from Windsor Castle to St. George's for her father's funeral, all the time getting off bawdy tales about Elizabeth I.

Students count on Miller to tell the truth. He always does. He pounds his desk extolling grit, integrity, and unstoppable dedication. They know he'll be there when they need wisdom or friendship.

Some parents call him a communist and demand that he be fired. Debates that begin in his classroom blaze into hallways and go home like torches to heat up family dinners. Miller takes stands on countless overlapping issues that divide students and parents and family and friends. He advocates Great Britain's "socialized medicine" in a room where Jeff Hatch, Leggy Williams, Isabel Wynne, Melissa Dee, Rodney Busch, Gabby Esmore, Cleo Richards, and Amy all have doctor fathers. "Eight of twenty-eight," Kathy calculates, "Call that 30 percent of our class."

---

[25] MN: Is this scene really in the Journal? Or did you copy it from JO's pages? Did Joe even take Miller's class?

    KN: Sure did! Best he ever had! If you'd read the Journal, you'd know.

After one dinner debate Leggy comes to class armed. "Look at the 'service,' all the 'prestige and power' of the American Medical Association."

Miller grins as he counters, "That's it. All that AMA 'power'! Tell us more about the 'service'! If emergency room doctors wore coin collectors on their belts like streetcar motormen we'd at least be able to count our change."

Carrie angles the conversation toward another red flag: "What about Joe McCarthy and his lists of 205, or sometimes 57, subversives according to his 'personal investigations'?"

Willie laughs, "McCarthy first made it to TV without a script. With the next program rolling live, 'Gunner Joe' ran around the studio asking everyone, 'What did I say? What did I say?'"

Washburn students consider themselves "Middle Class," some a bit more "Upper-" some a bit more "Lower-Middle." Washburn's few minorities are not poor: Kumalo and Hernando Graham's father is Minneapolis's first Black Superintendent of Schools. Art Robbins' father is a partner in a mostly Hispanic public interest law firm.

Walking from English to art class Amy tells Joe, "Come over to the house after dinner."

Joe looks at Amy in her full powder blue skirt and white sleeveless blouse. She tilts her head, waiting for his answer. He *wants* to go.

"Can't!" Joe finally says. "Kathy and I have to keep writing our show. I'm meeting her right after she tutors that genius 9th grader."

"How about that Deborah Ann Merkle?" Kathy says as she and Joe spread their script on her bed.[26] "She's something else!" Needing the money Kathy skips lunch three days a week to cross over to Ramsey, wondering why Deborah, with perfect A's, wants tutoring. "Thank God, next year with Hal Sheridan off to Conservatory at Oberlin, she'll take over the piano work for auditoriums. Gershwin can rest. The lightest music in Debbie's repertoire is Minotti. She told me her stomach turns over after four bars of 'An American in Paris' or 'Rhapsody in Blue.'"

---

[26] MN: How about that? You finally fell into a trap. You never tutored anyone like that, right?

KN: Well it's one way to slip in the kookiest material from Author (JO). Can't say I understand it. Do you? No, don't answer.

MN: Deborah Ann Merkle! You picked a pleasing name for your fictional tutelary.

KN: I'm the tutelary or tutor. She's the tutoree or pupil.

MN: Has three eyes, huh? Does she wear round heals"

KN: What?

MN: Does she go down easily?

Deborah asks Kathy, "Do you mind working with me?"

"Mind? Nothing else like it in my week."

"I recognize that I'm lightning fast and retentive and that turns some kids off. You know what I figured out last night? I calculated that the potential power of schooling starts when we recognize that each period, 30 students meet with a teacher for 50 minutes. Correct?"

"I'd count it that way."

"Most classes meet five times a day, five days a week—unless someone like Emily Berdseal vomits and the teacher sends everyone into the hall. Or doesn't that happen in high school?"

"Not as often. We've learned short cuts to the 'Girls' Room.'"

"During each 50-minute class—even if you assume that half the students are out of it—that leaves half for what I call 'A Learning Interaction.'"

"A Learning Interaction?"

"An Interaction means something learned. It can come from a single sentence, a whisper, a smile, or a note passed and received. Even if the note has nothing to do with school, learning's happening. Learning can be physical, like when one boy sneaks up behind me and bends down and another pushes me over so my books and pens and slide rule fly down the stairway. Or it can be intellectual, like when we find out that Napoleon invaded Russia and won the Battle of Borodino. By the way "The 1812 Overture" remains one of the few bombastic pieces I enjoy."

"Keep going."

"If half of the school's 1,200 students has only a single Learning Interaction each period, that sums to 600 Interactions. If most students take five classes, that totals 3,000 per day, per school."

"Sounds about right."

"The U.S. Department of Health, Education, and Welfare counts 24,000 secondary schools. Add up the Interactions—the discoveries—in a single day in all 48 states and you get 72 million chances. During a week you get 360 million. During a school year you get 14,400,000,000. Let's round that up to 15 billion opportunities for learning."

"Fifteen billion!"

"Well, in fairness, round it down to fourteen billion, which is low. But I guess we have to subtract for snow days, detentions, teachers' conferences—that sort of Mickey Mouse."

"Fantastic!"

"No, it's not! Don't you see all the wasted time? Schools miss so many opportunities. We have to stop all the nonsense and reconceive our whole educational system. Here! I wrote my calculations on the back of this score. Keep it. I seldom play Mendelssohn's "C Minor," and if I did I wouldn't need the score."

"Talk about Napoleon! You're a Revolutionary."

"Perhaps. But next year when I'm at Washburn, if you invite me to any of your parties, can you please make sure no one asks me to play popular songs? Without great orchestrations, music sucks. I'd be glad to help out with food, and I suppose I'd play if you can come up with any clean seventeenth- or eighteenth-century manuscripts. I like practically all classical music—unless it comes from Italy or Germany."

⌒⌐

Editor-in-Chief Woody Chesney charges into the *Grist* room shaking his curly head. "Hey! I just saw Mr. G. get into his car. The building's ours—except for the janitors, and they're on our side."

Mickey says, "Let's hit the basement. Louis Upson likes company. Maybe we can find the tunnel they say leads under the football field all the way to Ramsey."

Opening the door across from the stage marked "No Admittance," Woody and Mickey, with Doc, Leggy, Kathy, and Joe, descend a metal stairs to find the boiler room empty. Feeling along dark walls they locate a cave-like passage, mostly blocked by lawn equipment, bags of fertilizer, and boxes of towels and toilet paper.

Short of the passage Leggy spots light coming from a corner of the ceiling. Doc spots the ladder. Mickey scrambles up and at the top doesn't move.

Doc asks, "What do you see?"

"Nothing, right now, but I'm looking into a locker room I've never been in. One of those with coin machines on the wall."

"Mickey," Kathy says, "Has anyone said you were high-strung and dumb. *Not* a terrific combination."

Leggy asks, "Who would put a ladder here?"

"We probably shouldn't be here," Joe says.

"Right," Kathy says.[27]

---

[27]. KN: Everyone agreed it was not right, so each of us went up and down the ladder only once.

∽

Leaves battle outside the window on the landing above their homeroom. Joe checks the direction of the flag, planning to hit practice balls once he settles whatever's bothering Amy. Frowning and mute she sits on the ledge, her red flats with the straps swinging over radiator warmth. Homeroom teacher Hallam returns after a smoke in the boiler room with custodian Upson.

"Do you mind if I mark you both present?" he asks.

Joe says, "Okay, Mr. Hallam."

"If I didn't have a last period class or if you two took mechanical drawing I might ask to see your passes. You can go off and hit golf balls but how can I keep track of 30 kids every period, five periods a day? They don't even give me 30 drawing stools. That's why I let you lean on her desk in homeroom. That way I can keep track of you. That, and because I enjoy you. But believe me, 'Never go into teaching.'"

"I thought you *liked* it." Joe says.

"We don't teach; we fill out forms."

"You're good at it, Sir."

"Homeroom? Hardest period! Comes too early. So what do you kids plan for next year?"

"I suppose college," Joe says. "The U. Then do something worthwhile."

"Nothing's worthwhile! Find something you *like* to do. And forget about your hall passes. How would I know who signed them? Amy, I like your 'I Like Ike' button. Can't help but admire someone who'll dare to wear one of those in a school that's only 90 percent for the General. Don't let it poke a hole in your new lemon cashmere."

Amy snaps, "It's *not* new."

Going into his room Mr. Hallam says, "How do you expect me to keep track of 150 sweaters a day, five days a week, while I'm supposed to get idiots to draw decent arrowheads on their dimension lines?"

With the door to homeroom closed Joe wonders what Amy would do if he simply walked away to practice and left her on the ledge.

Her heel tests the radiator. Her lip sags. She doesn't notice the wind whipping the flag so hard its hardware chimes. He wants to slap or kiss her. "Do you still want to see *Hans Christian Andersen?*"

"Why wouldn't I?" She rolls the sleeves of her lemon sweater to her elbows and smoothes her over-the-knee kilt.

He'd like to twirl her out of both it and her mood. "Kathy says girls act different around the time of their...."

"Menstrual cycle? Curse?"

"She says Cleo has heavy cramps."[28]

"I don't have that! And I hope Kathy has Cleo's permission to provide her health history. Why does Kathy have to tell you so much?"

"Look, if I did something wrong I apologize."

"Don't apologize like some dumb bunny." Her voice and eyes go glassy enough to skate on. Above her white anklets she wears a Band-Aid. "You don't have to stay."

Joe slams the banister. He's built the kind of dream that materializes out of the mist every hundred years only to face an AMA doctor's daughter with another cashmere, a history book she never opens, and a belief that daddy and the Republican Party stand for "right," while striking teachers like Mr. Miller, socialized medicine, and kids without crew cuts like Mickey do not.

"I can't hit balls while you're like this, and *I* have to practice. I'm not like Doc. I'm not that good unless I work hard. I wish you'd work harder."

"At what?"

"At anything!"

---

28. MN: All that wisdom. I didn't know you had reached your monarchy by 11th grade.
KN: Menarche, pimple-breath! And it arrived in 6th grade on the Page Elementary playground.
MN: Along with the new swing set?

The bell rings; bodies bump; lockers bang; the halls feature wafts of uneaten egg salad. She turns away to stare out the window, away from kids pushing down the "Up" stairway.

Mr. Hallam reappears. "Glad to see you're having a good practice, or are you cutting that too?"

"I missed library completely," Amy says. "The librarian will send my name to the office."

Joe asks, "Could you maybe write Amy another pass? She had one from study hall, but didn't exactly use it."

"Is that my responsibility? Well I'd hate to see our assistant principal tattoo numbers on those delicate wrists." He bends close to Amy. "It's coming off you know. The spot by your mouth."

"It's not!"

"Thanks, Mr. Hallam," Joe says.

"Know what I'd do if I were you? Fly kites! Perfect afternoon. Plenty of breeze. Cut practice *and* library. In college you'll have too much studying to enjoy yourselves. Maybe even see each other." Hallam pushes the heavy bar on the 49th street doors. "Perfect day for kites!"

Amy arches her pelvis to push off the ledge, cradling her books in the soft wool. "I'm going to my locker. Come if you feel like it."

"What if I don't?"

"Maybe you should go fly a kite!"

He watches her kilted bottom start up the stair. "I'll call you after practice. I'm really late."

"Don't. I'll pick you up at the Nicollet streetcar stop."

"Are you kidding?"

"Why would I be kidding? Does Kathy kid you?"

"Okay, but I like it better when we take our car, not your mother's."

"I might let you drive."

He watches her climb past with the Band-Aid above her white socks and the red flats with the straps.

〜

Every spring Mickey waits anxiously for the Girls' Physical Education Department "Posture Contest." The week before he snuck into the room where they store mats and watched through the crack in the double doors as the girls in blue gym suits practiced walking in their high heels. Twelve hundred students fill the auditorium to focus on twelve finalists, four from each grade. Mr. Thompson sings "America the Beautiful" and then studies the card with the words to "We Love our Posture Queen," set by Hal Sheridan to the school fight song.

In the wings Miss Velma starts the girls, one at a time, across the stage. The first strolls. The second teeters on a chalked diagonal leading offstage into Washburn's blue velour curtains. The girls wear one-piece bathing suits with their heels, some carrying a towel, tennis racket, or other protective device to suggest casualness and keep them from tugging at their suits.

Two of the twelve eliminate themselves by hiding behind their towels. Carrie brings applause when she lobs a forehand high into the balcony where it bounces off the forehead of a small sophomore. Luther declares to Kathy that this is a superior auditorium program, "Much better than David Lean's film *Great Expectations* or the Mormon Boys' Band."

Six, including Frankie Hill, drop after answering, "What do you believe to be the most significant Washburn tradition?"

Four remain: a senior, defending Queen Jen Cummings, whose long hair could clean any boyfriend's clock or locker; a sophomore almost no one noticed filling her beakers in chem lab until her breasts began to fill and fill; Carrie; and, no surprise, Leggy Williams, who's always a finalist.

In homeroom Mr. Hallam lets Joe leave his stool in back to hang over Amy's drawing desk in front. For auditorium programs Hallam has assigned Joe and Amy seats on the left aisle of the front row next to each other.

Joe whispers to Amy, "They *all* look like they want to get offstage and back on their burger and Bridgeman's ice cream diets."

Mr. Thompson announces the breasted beaker girl as Third Runner-up; Leggy as Second Runner-up—a drop from last year; and Carrie as First Runner-up, leaving no one surprised that Jen Cummings becomes a repeat winner.

As the finalists march off, Amy looks out of place and embarrassed as Mr. Thompson starts, "We Love Our Posture Queen." Luther leans across her to say to Joe, "Of course we all know it's not how straight Jen stands, it's those nifty knockers."

Summer '52

On the final day of the Sheldon Memorial in Rochester, Mickey hits an eight-iron close to the flag on the twelfth, then takes three putts. He heaves his ball deep into the woods and his putter high into overhanging branches. His playing partners move to the next tee. Mickey keeps the group behind waiting while he climbs the tree, tears his trousers, and never posts a score.

Night rain slickens the blacktop as Mickey, still running hot, speeds them toward home. "Finger fucking, diddly gash. I told you it wouldn't go in if they didn't grow hair around the cup."

"What did he say?" Joe asks Doc.

"He said he didn't use enough club on that second putt."

Mickey ignores the slipperiness, braking and fishtailing on smooth-treaded tires. Joe and Doc make him pull over at a diner.[29]

The waitress looks as though she's worked three shifts. Mickey tries to joke with her as she takes their orders and ignores him. He pulls a packet from his pocket and places it on the table. "Do you think she'd like this?"

[29.] MN: We played a lot of tournaments around the state for three summers, but this one and its post-round fete do not go down as my proudest. At least, though, I was the only one to ask the waitress when she last washed her hands, a state requirement according to the sign posted in the can.

Looking at the foil, Joe says, "I do *not* think she would like that. She's probably married or has a boyfriend."

The girl carries their platters with burgers and fries, a catsup bottle tucked under one arm.

"So, you going out with anyone this summer?" Joe asks Doc.

"Like to ask Leggy. Same height, but she dances better."

"Don't forget what everyone thought in 9th grade," Mickey says. "I couldn't get Kathy or the other FEMS to open up, but they suspected that Leggy and Jeff were doing it."[30]

When they finish their burgers, Mickey offers to leave the tip. That surprises Doc and Joe, but they head for the door. Looking back they see Mickey unrolling a rubber over the catsup bottle.

Standing in a downpour Joe tells Mickey, "You'll feel a hell of a lot better if you go back and wipe that into a napkin. Think what Frankie would say."

"Frankie's not here. Girls go for surprises."

"That's more than a surprise," Doc says.

"You want a ride home or not?"

"Not necessarily," Doc says, "Just tote our clubs to town."

"I'll be home before you."

"Probably," Joe says as he picks up his duffel where he packed a photo of Adlai Stevenson with a hole in his shoe for Kathy and one of abdicating King Farouk that he autographed, "With love to Mickey, my best big buddy."

"Up to you," Mickey says starting the engine. "Tough hitchhiking in the dark in the rain."

Inside the diner the girl moves as slowly as she likely does in school, if she is still goes to school. They return to the same table and order coffee and pie. "Like big-deal truckers," Doc says.

When they leave, the bottle top is on, cleaner than it's been all summer.

---

30. KN: We never knew. And she paid for that, forced to run the rim of a rumor. We did wonder at the time whether Leggy was acting different—as though she knew something we didn't.

Mr. Baxter dies the day Doc wins his quarterfinal match in the Pine to Palm Tournament at Alexandria, beating Southwest's Jim Raleigh. A heart attack! No warning!

As soon as he hears, Joe heads down the hills to Amy's and they debate whether to drive to Doc's. They can't decide, so they never leave the basement, but next morning Amy calls around to collect for flowers from Bachman's Nursery.

Luther and Kathy join Amy and Joe to deliver the plant. Doc's older brother comes to the door, thanks them, but does not invite them in.

In the car behind his Clark Kent glasses, big wooly-haired Luther looks teary and Kathy cries. Amy doesn't, which makes Joe wonder.

~

"You mean Tom Heggen lived two blocks from here?" Joe says. "Down your alley and less than a block south? I want to see."

Amy sits on a pylon on the humped footbridge over the Minnehaha Creek, tan below a blue Oxford shirt and white shorts. She lets a loafer hang precariously over the summer trickle. "Daddy says he lived longer over by Southwest."

"What street?"

"How badly do you want to know? Daddy's got both addresses. One on Portland, one on Beard." She leans back; pine needles stick to her, and her collar opens wider.

"Your father's shirt's almost as loose as your 'dating blouse.' Remember you called it that because it was 'less fuss to take off.'"

"You're making that up."

"You were there. And here when you lean back you *do* look a little lopsided."

"Every girl is, silly. One side's usually smaller than the other, even when they're...more generous. Look at Liz Taylor—beauty mole included. When Leggy and I were little we'd shop and joke about who was ready for a 'Freshman' or 'Little Angel.' Imagine putting your arms into 'Support to start your development.' No, thank you. And I don't think this is a dating blouse. It can't be. This is *not* a date; it's afternoon."

"So get your round rear off the pine needles. Let's go see."

She shuts her eyes and reaches for an overhanging branch. "I can't see. Not sun. Not sky. But I can see you. I must be blinded by beauty, so I won't be able to see the house were Tommy lived."

"Thomas! Or just Tom."

"Respect for the dead?"

"For a damned fine novelist and playwright."

"One book and he goes po-oo-f." She releases a maple pod so it swivels toward the pebbly bridge. When she reaches for another, her finger catches a splinter. "Ouchies! And gooies!" She wipes blood dots on her shorts, but peels another pod and spreads its flaps over her nose. "See? Pinocchio! I must have told a fib. Do you like me…lying—or is it laying?"

"Do you have a mark on your rear like the nurse in Tom's play?"

"That dirty play? Sweaty sailors. All that swearing. Nasty, nasty! All that talk about nurses taking showers. And they didn't say 'rear'; they shouted about 'a birthmark on her ass.'"

She skips across the grassy slope. They cross the Parkway, Tarrymore Avenue, and the half-block to her alley on 51st. They climb past the house set back from the street and the vacant lot to her garage.

"I can get mom's car."

"To go two blocks?"

"I'd let you drive. And we might want to swing around Pearl Field, past Diamond Lake, and park where Hampshire dead ends."

"You're the one who said it's afternoon. Not a date!"

"It's later now."

"We'll walk. Heggen said all Midwest houses look alike, and the people are bigots."

"I are small. And wasn't he always hung over?"

"He didn't have many years to be hung over."

"If daddy isn't home we can ask Rosemary. You're gonna like her. She's only twenty-eight and knows everything about making babies—or not making them. More than Kathy knows, I bet."

Amy leans over the latticed fence around the garden where her father's roses are staked in red rows and labeled.

"Why get on Kathy?"

"Rosemary had her first baby at eighteen. For me that would mean winter after next—when we'll be college freshmen. Her husband travels all the time. He's got a widow's peak like yours, but no dimples."

"You don't make babies long distance with dimples."

Amy pokes a finger into her cheek. "Da-ah! She had to have a C-Section on the last, like Liz Taylor. She knows all about eastern colleges too. The East would be fun—although I'm hoping we can go down and hold hands for four years at Carleton."

"I'm going to the U. You should too."

"Rosemary says Carleton's okay, but Smith's better for me, Yale or Princeton for you. She's dated guys from each and says my hips are perfect for...."

"Don't start that again. It's afternoon! What am I supposed to feel?"

"My hips maybe? Clean white shorts? Neato huh?"

He unlatches the gate. "I don't see your dad."

"He said he was coming home to play with his flowers. Hey, Rosemary." Amy waves at the woman in the next yard unfolding a playpen. "Rosemary, you remember Joe. And vice versa, right? We're going to Heggen's."

Rosemary's voice sounds puffed like her belly. "A new drive-in?"

Joe explains, "It's one of the houses where Thomas Heggen lived when he went to the U. He was in the navy and wrote *Mr. Roberts*—one of the best World War II books. Definitely the shortest and funniest."

Amy plucks an envelope from a rose stake. "Ouch! Dad says it's '5117 Portland.' Diamond Lake Lutheran's '5760' so figure the East Side. We'll ride the Raleigh. But first, something cool."

Joe wants to hold Amy and rub the flakes peeling from her nose as he follows in the side door.

They sit in her father's den with a pitcher of iced tea and point at pictures and tickle. She finds the page showing variations on the female organs and asks, "Okay, smart guy, which one do you think is me?"

"Not the canoe?"

"Not the canoe or the wigwam. I'm not even on the page, Dumbo. I'd never let them take a picture of me. Come on! Upstairs!"[31]

Amy leads him to her room. They know her folks trust them. They also know her folks might appear any moment. She kicks off her loafers and they lie hugging on her bed, but only briefly, touching mostly above the waist, mostly outside their clothing. He knows the risk of going this far. In her room. On her bed.

"I guess I'm not supposed to check for canoes or wig-wams," he says.

"Not now. That's why mummy and daddy want me wearing clothes. Except when I take a bath or when they're not necessary."

Back outside Amy, still barefoot, drags out the fat-tired Raleigh. They push it to the head of the alley to take advantage of the decent. She insists that he sit on the handlebars while she swings a leg over, banging herself on the boy's bar. The bike wavers as it rolls. Her legs are not long enough, so she stands, causing them to sway, almost tipping.

They pick up speed on the lower slope, barreling by her garage into the middle of 51st. With no cars passing, she's able

---

[31] MN: Okay, Kate the Great, you're his biggest fan. What's the worst thing Good Boy Joe ever did?

KN: Back in high school? I suppose the night eating at the Hasty Tasty at 50th and France after another movie where Susan Hayward dies. Cleo suggested we all order the same thing to make it easy for the waitress. Joe asked them to add lettuce and tomato to his.

MN: Geez, what a shitty thing to do.

KN: When everyone came down on him, he agreed to leave off the lettuce and tomato, but said, "No problem, I'd do the same for a white man."

MN: So?

KN: He was sitting with Kumalo and Art Robbins, Black; Luther, Jewish; and Cleo, Kathy, Carrie, Amy, and me, five females. Cleo patted his head and said, "Joe, dear, you're the only truly white male eating burgers. Would you prefer we move to another table?"

MN: Did his white face get paler?

KN: Couldn't tell. He slid under the table.

to jog the handlebars left, where the alley continues behind the houses in the next block, Luverne curving into Portland just south of the creek and Parkway.

Seeing her try to drag a foot he considers jumping to stop them. But as they near her mother's rented garage she bangs the brakes, throwing herself over the handlebars, chin sliding over concrete, a bare foot tangling in the chain.

Wiping a hand on her shorts, she lets him help her up. "This isn't all my blood. Some's yours and some's grease from the chain."

"Which is which?"

"I can feel the difference."

"I hate to see you hurt."

"Then don't come into the operating room. Rosemary says having a baby's bloodier than falling off a bike—or the roof."

He walks the bike. She limps along down the curving alley until it joins Portland, where they start south. Traffic rushes north toward downtown; fewer cars drift south toward the cattails of Diamond Lake. "Daddy said to look for the house with lilac bushes."

He takes her hand. "Let's cross."

"Are you taking me to the land where they keep the odd-numbered houses?"

"Kathy said he lived here the summer his family moved up from Iowa and he commuted to the U. Terrible grades and lots of parties. Lost the tip of his finger playing a joke with big newspaper scissors."

Amy moves ahead, walking the curb like a high wire. Joe counts houses, figuring the one they want will be the last on the straightaway or the first where Portland splits with a service road. "I know you don't like me saying it, but I've learned a lot from Kathy. But she's…well, I don't think of her so much as a girl."

"Doesn't she wear a bra or get a period? Any of those neat things?"

Amy suddenly sits down on the curb, wrapping her arms around her knees.

Joe says. "We don't have to mention her. She's a...wonderful person, but I've never wanted to grab for her all the time like I do you."

"You grab and I'll stop the first car."

"And say what?"

She grins. "That I want to make a 'Citizen's Arrest.' I'll say you're a sailor who hasn't seen a girl so long you've lost control. Why didn't you grab me back at the bridge?"

"Because."

"That's a Modess ad."

"You might have squirmed away and made me feel silly. I worry that sometime I'll reach out and you won't be there."

"I worry about that too."

He touches her shoulder. A woman looking out her window raps on the glass. Amy breaks a stick and holds out two ends. "Pick one. If you get the longer one, you can stop worrying about me." He opens his hand. Her stick is longer.

Their lips touch. A Pontiac honks and he wants to give it the finger. Amy's scowl softens, nose rubbing against the grease on both faces. "I'd invite you to shower with me and bandage my leg, but if daddy's watering the garden the pressure will be too low."

They stop at a blue-trimmed stucco under two elms with lilacs rising to the windows. Joe pictures a young Ensign sitting on a Studebaker trunk, studying the lilac and coming up with his idea for the Captain's palm tree. "I could sob like a kid every time Pulver reads the letter saying Roberts' plane has crashed. And cheer every time he stirs himself up to bang on the Captain's cabin and yell that he's going to throw the Goddamn palm tree overboard. Although they only say 'damn' in the touring company."

"I've never seen you cry. 'Tape me up and send me back in. That's you."

"You didn't tear up when you hurt your leg. *Mr. Roberts* was still running on Broadway with Henry Fonda when Heggen ran water in a New York hotel bathtub and ran a razor across his wrists."

"Nothing they could bandage, huh? I don't think I'll bandage my leg either. That would make a bulge under my summer stockings. They're new and very sneaky: they only come up to my knees, so my skirt covers the top. Clever? No one can tell where they stop."

"I'll know. Get on the seat. I'm pedaling us back."

"I'll sit and whisper to your wispy neck hairs. Just don't bounce me."

Sensing her legs open around him he pumps up the alley, almost making it to her garage. "Still got the hots?" she whispers as her father comes from the shed with a sprayer.

The doctor says, "Glad to see you've got him pedaling. Basketball players need to build the legs."

"Daddy! He's not the basketball one."

"Wrong one? Terrible to find you're operating on the wrong one. Sorry, Joe. How *are* your legs?"

"Fine, Sir." Joe checks the scrape along Amy's tan, below the dirt and grease on her white shorts and shirttails. "We found Heggen's house."

"No reason you wouldn't," the doctor says. "Correct address, fine Raleigh, a very good guide, plus the push you got from Amy's friend. Kathy, is it?"

"Daddy!"

"And am I mistaken in thinking that Raleigh's both the brand of bike and the name of one of the young men who's called here?"

Amy starts for the house. "Don't be a tease."

The doctor watches her go, turning to Joe. "You played a good round. I figure you covered four blocks in two hours. Lucky you didn't break a chain and have to walk back."

〜

KN: Can't you run this one with someone else, weenie?

MN: You're the only one who knows the lines, nerdball. Let's go, we're talking "missed opportunity." We're talking Joe, almost a senior with a whole world ahead of him....

KN: ...to let me help plan a brilliant future....

MN: ...left alone with the doctor's medical library. Amy upstairs dressing. By the by I don't think he missed her meaning about canoes and wigwams.

KN: Oh, no! I suppose though after she went upstairs he might have *glanced* again inside a book or two— maybe thumbed the colored plates.

MN: I imagine the FEMS spent many an instructional hour closeted in the good doctor's den while matriculating up the hill at Page. So there we have Joe: surrounded by pictures of body parts.

KN: I bet he didn't browse much.

MN: He must have noticed a few titles. Perhaps the sequel to *My Gynecologist, Your Gynecologist.*

KN: Only the first half of that has illustrations; the rest is footnotes—and you know how the casual reader feels about *that* scholarly apparatus. It *is* unfair, though, that they photograph so many more details of girls.

MN: Doesn't matter. From a distance it all looks the same.

KN: I guess that *is* as close as you get.

MN: When we were wee ones I guess I shouldn't have shown mom that Big Little Book where Dagwood Bumstead sucks off Tillie Tyler.

KN: Well porn's more than a cottage industry now.

MN: Can't you picture Joe rushing to push a book back on the shelf when her sweet feet descended the stairs....

KN: Not in her daffodil gown.

MN: ...and finding he'd shoved the book back upside down.

KN: I bet she wore clean white shorts every day that summer.

MN: With merely a "dating blouse" to keep it simple. Only two pieces of clothing to remember.

KN: Four! You forgot her underwear.

MN: So did she.

Fall '52

They cross from the *Grist* room, Kathy carrying the standing lamp from her bedroom. She opens the door into the dark backstage space, pushing around velour side curtains. "We need to find a plug."

"Last winter a window pole, this time a floor plug," Joe says.

"On your knees, lackey. Feel near downstage center. Downstage's there!" In the light from the single bulb Kathy faces the mouth of the auditorium. "This is the way they do auditions on Broadway."

"Are we auditioning or writing a show for the newpaper staff?"

"We're conceiving. You know what that means, right? We need focus."

"You focus, I'll follow."

"Minimal scenery."

"We're doing Thornton Wilder?"

"Better than that! We'll lay a track across the stage here and hang an S-shaped curtain. That way we can get one scene ready to slide on before the other scene ends. Continuous action. All flow. A bare stage with a few prop pieces, but mostly our singers and dancers—if we can find anyone with a voice besides Jeff and Leggy. Oh, and we need a Greek chorus."

"To do what?"

"Talk! To the audience and to the characters. How's this? We tell a story about a guy like you—named Joseph Taylor, Jr. He goes off to medical school, marries a loose woman, gets lured by rich patients, and finally meets a nurse who talks him into going home. Pretty good, huh? His dead grandmother sings, telling him to come home. I can do that. Grandmothers sit a lot and you can do Joe because he doesn't have to sing much."

"Didn't we see this at the Lyceum? The third Rodgers and Hammerstein? The one you worshipped?

"I worship beauty. So what if someone recognizes bits here and there? And we have to get our music from some show. We'll write our own words—mostly."

"And you'll direct."

"I thought perhaps I might. We'll make it wonderful. Something dizzy and new."

"Yeah, *Allegro*. Instead, how about writing down what we remember from *Oklahoma!*? The old woman churning butter in front of a backdrop of cornfields. The baritone offstage telling us what a beautiful morning it is. His girl inside the farmhouse waiting for her cue so she can make her entrance and tease him. We can even leave off the exclamation mark so our *Oklahoma* will seem more original."

KN: Come in Michael! Do you read me? It's school history time.

MN: Oh, my buns get hot for history time.[32]

KN: Washburn tradition extends to the century's first quarter. By 1926 the Crosby family had ground so much flour they wanted to give something back. They grew a school and planted Poplar Row—with funds to replace any trees that died. And of course they mounted in the front hall that peculiar bronze bust of first Principal McQuarrie.

MN: Remember how you'd put your back against the wall on one side and lock on McQuarrie's profile. Keeping your eyes on the face you'd walk around watching the profile until you got to the other side.

KN: And the nose would move, right?

MN: Like a bull's cock.

KN: That spot was like the Pantheon.

MN: A shrine where you could stand across the dome and hear tourists fart.

KN: We'll skip over the mashed potatoes and gravy the cafeteria served Fridays with elephant balls, but did you know that Washburn did not begin with a senior class. The first group ruled until they graduated in 1927, the year we killed Sacco and Vanzetti, sat a bunch of Black kids in the electric chair, and cheered with 80,000 in the new Yale Bowl.

MN: Lucky that Amelia was flying the Pacific and never heard about that.

KN: Better hold your note cards closer; I can see that you're going to claim Hal Sheridan really composed "An American in Paris."

---

[32] MN: Thank you very much Mr. Author (JO) for interrupting Joe's story with your early 50's material.

MN: When Washburn was young, you'd look over a hill through woods to try to see Nicollet Avenue. No McQuarrie Field. No Ramsey on the corner of 49th.

KN: Later: the Hennepin County Orphanage huddled on the streetcar line.

MN: Handy for the little ones when they wanted to ride downtown to shop.

KN: Washburn didn't have a principal when it opened. McQuarrie gave it two years to get it on track and stayed five. The first real principal, Vail Allerton, took the helm in 1930 and no one saw him leave his office for fifteen years. Our Vallon Van Husen walked into a vacuum.

MN: Did he ever do anything?

KN: He presided over the last mid-year graduating class in 1949. He integrated boys and girls in home-rooms, lunchroom, and the auditorium.

MN: Any success with co-ed rest rooms?

KN: All these years Washburn flourished because of its code: Middle Class social justice combined with nonviolence, equality, a touch of diversity, and reasonable sexuality.

MN: Bet a buck you won't say what's reasonable.

KN: Girls could use dirty words but they had to act polite.

MN: A teacher didn't need to worry about losing a favorite fountain pen or discovering confetti and syrup in a tampon tube.

KN: Academic freedom blanketed the school.

MN: Willie Miller didn't kick me out of class when I suggested printing a boxed edition of *Sensuality and Sensibility* along with *Pride and Pudenda*.

KN: Don't tell me! For sixty-nine cents!

MN: Enough history? Let's check out the boiler room. Maybe we can sneak a smoke and see if they ever patched that hole in the ceiling.

KN: Floor!

MN: Depends on which way you're trying to look. Why didn't Leggy tell Joe when Amy went out with someone else?

KN: Why didn't you?

MN: Chickenshit, I guess. Let's waltz once around the bust of McQuarrie and hit 'em with a closer.

KN: Fire away, little fellow.

MN: Are you ready for this one?

KN: I'm vamping. Get it right this time.

MN: Here we go: "Do you think McQuarrie was his real name?"

KN: (Pause.) "Whose real name?"

MN: Blackout![33]

[33.] MN: When you grow up two doors away from him and one thin wall from her plaster cast you often want to pound the shit out of them. Joe could be so good at being good. Mom and *Robin Big Breasts* saw him that way. But some days I saw him as pious, stubborn, and the toughest opponent anyone faced when he defended my sister—which was *always*.

KN: A nice boy. Mr. Midwest Everyboy, 1952.

MN: Jones 252-232.

KN: What's that mean?

MN: Don't have the foggiest. It's scrawled in the corner of a JO page. Actually it says, "Dow-Jones: High 252-Low 232." And under that he's written, "I did get something...a little cocker spaniel dog." The name "Richard M. Nixon" is written in after that. I remember him. And JO wrote, "Female card-holders are required to show their loyalty to the cause through indiscriminate intercourse where it will do the most good."

KN: Heavens, that's all?

MN: Oh, he's added the words, "USA Confidential—on the C.P."

KN: "C.P."?

MN: Cun....

KN: Don't go any further! This material does not matter.

MN: How about Joe McCarthy's, "You can't fight Communism with perfume"?

KN: I've retired from the ring.

∽

Mickey's taking up all the couch space and Jud and Luther slump in chairs finishing a beer and opening another when former *Grist* editor Woody Chesney calls Kathy from Harvard. After digressions about the Hasty Pudding Show and drinking beer at Cronin's down from the Square, Woody says he wants to pin her and wants advice about going for one of the Final Clubs—probably not Porcellian, maybe Fly or Delphic.

When Joe arrives and turns down Mickey's offer of a beer, Kathy's still on the phone to Cambridge saying, "No, I don't think you should. They're a whole lot worse than Washburn's only sorority and fraternity, SOROSIS and MARS, and you wrote editorials against them."

When Kathy hangs up Luther announces, "Now for a little local politicking. We need to change class officers. And I speak as one of them."

"No kidding!" Kathy says, still irritated.

"I can line up the guys. How about you Kathy; can you count on the girls?"

"Class officers?" Mickey asks. "Are those the ones that never talk to you in the halls, but want you to applaud when they run down the field?"

"Who you thinking of running?" Kathy asks.

Luther looks down modestly. "I seem to be no more than perpetual vice-presidential timber. How 'bout if I don't run and we campaign super speed for Carrie Browne?"

"Carrie?" Kathy asks.

Joe says, "I think she'd like to be an officer. But do we want Jeff to drop into Luther's spot?"

Luther sets down his bottle. "Why not Carrie for president and Kathy for veep? Let Jeff battle it out for secretary."

"Tough cob!" Joe says, "but Jeff's got the athletes and MARS fraternity guys. Also the pretty little girls who don't say much."

"That's the point of a free election," Luther says. "Last night at Leggy's she and Cleo said they'd vote for change. Let's push for it."

Joe asks, "Did they know how much change you're rattling?"

Kathy says, "Carrie won't get all the huggy-bear votes you get, Luther."

"Why not run Doc?" Mickey suggests.

"Not political enough," Kathy answers.

"Well par-don me! The guy hits the ball a ton." Mickey leans back and turns on the radio for the Joe Walcott-Ezzard Charles bout. Mickey's the only one rooting for Charles. "Jersey Joe's gotten too old—and slow."

As Gillette Blue Blades bring the bout into the Nolan living room, Kathy trails the phone cord around the corner to call Leggy. When she returns she's decided to turn down Woody's pin, whether he gets it from a Final Club or buys it from a posh shop off Harvard Square and Mickey's taken a blow to the gut by betting against the world's oldest heavy weight champ.

〜

Jeff's father drives five jittery classmates to Eland Hall at the U to take the College Boards: the three-hour Aptitude in the morning and three Achievement Tests in the afternoon. Joe feels Amy on his lap, but has no sensation that this is like a date.

Registration for the SAT begins at 8 a.m., with the reading of instructions lasting almost an hour. Finally, with number two pencils poised, they hear the order, "Begin!"

After a half-hour to get their answer sheet and test booklets checked in, they're given a lunch break. They cross the snowy mall in front of Northrop Auditorium to the cafeteria in Coffman Memorial Union.

Back in the windowless basement room, Joe takes Achievement Tests in mathematics, English Composition, and Spanish. When they finally resurface at ground level, Joe's surprised to find them exiting the ancient building into darkness.

Leggy says, "Math was hardest." Jeff and Luther agree that any multiple choice test is less challenging and easier than writing a paper. Amy says that when she wasn't sure she blackened the "C" space. Joe admits that on several math items he started with one of the answers and calculated backwards, a slow and unscientific process.

Kathy says, "Too much about college depends on these crappy tests."

Cleo says, "Yeah, and we have to come back in March for Achievements in courses we're taking now. And they'll never even tell us our scores. Only whether a college admits us or doesn't."

Jeff says, "I'm going to take advanced math in May— even though we'll know by then which colleges want us."

"Luther is too," Mrs. Stern says as she drives them back to South Minneapolis where Mrs. Johnson has a late supper waiting. Afterwards Joe falls asleep on the sofa in Amy's basement. Earlier they'd planned to park at Lake Harriet to watch the submarine races.[34]

---

[34] MN: Variations of which still exist, but nothing like the row of cars angled toward the lake on the east shore down from the Rose Gardens, which also provided its overflow rectangle for late arrivers.

KN: My sources tell me that by then Joe and Amy had begun avoiding anything public in favor of private retreats. Their favorite: where Hampshire Drive comes south off Diamond Lake, curves along the west side of Pearl Park, thus housed on only one side, coming to a dead end circle behind somebody's garages and bushes.

MN: Parked there, facing back on Hampshire, they could see any approaching car a long ways away.

KN: Precisely! A perfect make-out spot.

MN: Which they learned to use to perfection.

Winter '53

In 11th grade English Mr. Miller would never give Joe a mark below "A." Now in 12th grade Miss Marsh has blotted the report card of the Editor-in-Chief of the *Grist* with a "B."

Joe stays after class and asks, not too politely, "What do you want us to do in here?"

"What do you want to do?" Miss Marsh asks.

"You never give much homework. And during class you don't seem to care if we talk or pass around notes."

"Don't you expect to talk and write all your life?"

"I don't understand."

"I didn't think so. After college, do you picture yourself getting grades and having teachers keeping you from whispering and passing notes?"

"What's that have to do with English class?"

"Would you feel better if I assigned you a research paper?"

"Would that bring my mark up?"

"What would you like to learn? What truly interests you?"

"Musical shows. I usher for all of them that come to the Lyceum—see the same show, maybe, 16 times during the two weeks it's in town, six nights and Wednesday and Saturday matinees. I check out scores from the downtown library—even though I can't read music, only lyrics and the book."

"Have you tried to go backstage to interview, say, Elaine Strich—she was here in *Call Me Madam*, wasn't she? Or Allan

Jones in the Robert Alda part in *Guys and Dolls*? Did you know Jones sang in the 1936 film of *Show Boat* with Paul Robeson?"

"That doesn't sound like school work."

"All right. Write me a paper about 'Existentialism.'"

"What's that?"

"Check out books like you do on musicals. I'll start you by saying it has to do with 'essence' and 'existence.' Have you heard of Camus? Sartre? The hydrogen bomb?"

"I suppose I can give it a try."

"Start anywhere, and see where you end up."

Knowing Amy will be mad if she hears about it, Joe skips his Hi-Y meeting at Albright's to sit on the Nolan's front steps. Kathy's upset that Woody Chesney really wants to put himself in position for an invitation from Fly. "That's the Final Club FDR started when he was turned down by Porcellian." She urges Joe to collaborate on a tough editorial against Washburn's sorority and fraternity, SOROSIS and MARS. She's slightly uneasy though about how that will look because neither she nor Joe has been asked to join.

She takes Joe to her room and shows him the draft of a petition calling for a complete disbandment of both secret clubs before the end of this, their graduation year.

"Do you think you have the votes?" Joe asks. "Where's Leggy stand? She's the one FEM in SOROSIS."

"I'm working on her. She's crucial. If she agrees, we've got Cleo and Amy for sure. Carrie naturally supports disbandment."

Although Joe's never been too bothered about not being asked to join MARS, he feels uncertain as he walks home. But he realizes that Kathy's probably right. She usually is.

〜

Frankie Hill has needed a secretary to schedule her ever since she crossed over from Ramsey two years ago. Yet Mickey has never managed to move much beyond leering and throwing spitballs.[35] As a junior, Frankie's started going out with heavy hitters. She's the first girl Doc Baxter has gotten serious about, even though his Missouri Synod Lutheran parents are raising so many questions about her Catholicity that Doc will probably wave a white flag and go back to cruisin' with the guys.

When Jeff Hatch makes his move everyone pays attention. Though it's been three years since the 9th grade rumors about him and Leggy, everyone feels protective about Frankie. She's their gymnast, cheerleader, their quiet girl with all the talent. She's so cute.

Kathy asks, "Why would she go from a solid All-City quarterback to a grade-grubbing tennis player on the make. He's one slick prick. Why has he been our class president every year since Luther in 9th grade?"[36]

Kathy and Joe know dating rituals. When doubling with another couple, the driver has the advantage of dumping the backseat pair, and using the remaining time as he, she, or their parents allow. However the backseat during a double date leaves more hands free. Most agree that during a first date you should not stretch for oral lip-to-lip contact, certainly not for "bare earlobe."

---

[35] MN: And jacking off—although no one marketed that concept back then.

[36] KN: No one in our class was more likeable and kinder than Luther Stern.

MN: And no one could get Luther back to Jules Barbershop. He wouldn't put up 75¢ to get sanded around the ears by a bastard who held the clippers to your skull and spun the chair. A bastard who made any kid wait when the honorable Mr. Adult strolled in. A bastard who made cracks about anyone with a name that might sound Jewish—like Stern.

Joe and Kathy worry whenever they watch Frankie ride off with Jeff. Although whenever that happens, Joe at least knows there's no way Jeff's out with Amy.[37]

---

[37] KN: I never wrote this part. God, I would never mention earlobes. I wouldn't even admit to having them if I didn't have to shampoo my hair regularly and wrap it in a towel. As for dumping the backseat couple: I never ranked high on the chart of "Had the Most Dates," but I sure had some where an early drop, like halfway from the diner to my house, would have been fine. My hot pursuit came from a mind much hotter than hands. Woody?... Well, you get the idea.

Spring '53

The car radio finishes pumping out "Come on-a My House." Then Gary Cooper strides down the dusty street to confront the men coming to gun him down while the orchestra plays the theme from "High Noon"—the tune Ike whistles in the White House.

Amy's face hints Tabu in strands of lemon, as her tongue darts against his.

Joe wraps himself around her, keeping her head from scraping the icy window or bumping the steering wheel. "Spoons! We're making spoons," she squeals, as his knees bend behind hers, shivering and clamping. His hands slide inside the scoop of her blouse where he tries to enclose her completely.[38]

"Do you like my dating blouse?" she purrs. "It's your fault it got this way. You stretched it. All that mad grabbing."

His fingers work where the band hooks across her back.

"I guess you don't know how to do it. Girls learn these things early. The hook opens and the nylon loosens and lands on the dashboard. Mouths move more; blondness tangles; sweetness spreads. She unties a velvet ribbon, hair hanging straight as he rubs her legs.

---

[38] KN: I grew up with her and talked late into many nights with him. Yet I tried not to picture them alone together. And when my chance finally came at the Radisson Hotel, I blew it.

"Do I need shaving?" He feels her warmth and fullness. As the radio slides in with the Lavender Blue song he wonders how he'll ever get enough of her. He rolls so their faces and hips lock. She pushes her toes against the door, using her fists to help wriggle out of her shorts. She hugs and moves against him. They press into each other. For the first time, his hand touches the silk below her waist.

A band of elastic. He stops. He waits for a reaction. When she doesn't move his hand he lets it slide under. It crosses a smooth rise to find itself at a curly edge.

"What's the matter?" she asks, twisting but not moving away.

"It's neat."

"It?"

"Can't you feel it?"

"I feel your hand lower than where my appendix used to be. Did I say you could touch that low?"

"Sorry. It's so soft. Furry."

"Well it all happens to be me. And you only have to say you're sorry the first time. So you're done with that necessity. We might as well make it easier. Tug!"

She arches so he can stretch her waist elastic and pull. He floats a second silk toward the dashboard.

His fingers fall lower and twine. "Oh, I so…." He whispers, "I really think I do…love you, I mean."[39]

She sighs and grunts.

After a long time, Amy reaches over him. Without putting on her underwear, she pulls up her shorts and puts her arms through the holes in her blouse, buttoning every other one. She looks dainty and sure: significant enough to die for. She wipes her mouth and his with the back of her hand. She stretches to grab her clothes from the dashboard. When he tries to help she pushes him away, balling her bra and panties and stuffing them into her purse. Something to wash in the upstairs sink rather than drop down the chute with the regular laundry.

[39.] KN: Joe's Journal dissolves from sentences into notes—squiggly marks. So his words here are sometimes guesses.

⌒⌒

"I'll drive you home," Kathy says when Frankie wants to skip the cast party. Frankie still wears makeup on her neck from *A Midsummer Night's Dream* as Kathy drives east along Minnehaha Creek.[40] It's icy and the car almost skids where the Parkway rises and curves past Portland.

Frankie says, "I worry some car will come out a side street and do that 'slip-in and slow-down-in-front-of-you thing.'"

Past Chicago the creek widens and swirls with debris, stretching all across South Minneapolis from Lake Minnetonka to the Mississippi River, gaining power with the additional flow from Lake Harriet. Ahead at Bloomington Avenue they see flashing red from police cars. Kathy pulls over. "John Law better not write out a ticket. Our Shakespeare wasn't that bad."

They walk where melting snow floods walking paths and grassy strips from street to creek. The main currents cause branches to crack and tree limbs to leap, not like the feeble flow that will drop over the Falls to the Mississippi come late summer.

A boy has fallen through the ice thirty yards upstream. Someone heard him call out, but he's been cut by the ice and carried to here before disappearing underneath.

Kathy and Frankie stand near warning signs where flood-lights hit the water and jagged ice wedges rise over the banks and firemen work with axes and harpoon-like picks.

"I'd like to go home," Frankie says. "Is that okay?"[41]

"Sure! But is everything really okay? I guess I mean with Jeff."

"He dropped me. He said he wanted to play the field. He said he wanted to start with your friend Amy."[42]

---

40. KN: She played Helena and destroyed the balance of the play. Demetrius and Lysander, and the actors who played them—Jeff and Doc—and the audience fell so in love with her, that Cleo as Hermia got really lost in the woods on that summer night near Athens.

41. MN: God, what a looker! Biggest little boobs not-yet-in-captivity!

42. KN: I never could decide what to make of Frankie. I felt a sadness about her, more than a joy. The beautiful doll. Cheerleader, gymnast, epileptic. I thought Joe used her to measure his relationship with Amy. I always thought Amy might jump one way and Joe another. Toward Frankie.

The auditorium's packed for the Pep Rally. All three grades are required to cheer on the basketball team in its fight to go from its District Championship, through the Regionals, and maybe to the State Tournament at the University's Williams Arena. Hal Sheridan opens the program by banging out "An American in Paris." Several teachers risk their lives in front of 1,500 Miller fans. Toby Thompson leads the crowd in "Cheer for the Orange and Blue" to the tune of Yale's "Down the Field," going solo when no one knows the last verse. Teacher *Señorita* Jan Dahlquist knocks everyone out with an animated act no one understands because she speaks Spanish with a Swedish accent. Principal Van Husen reads the same notes as last year about safe driving, and reminds everyone, "Never forget for a moment that out there you're the face of this school." Hal Sheridan returns with "Rhapsody in Blue."

"I think he's playing it over again," Amy whispers to Joe.

When the music ends, Mr. G. intones, "You may now return to your third period class."

The call comes late. Joe's folks are asleep when Kathy says, "Don't spread this around, but she's going to need close friends."

"What's wrong?"

"Frankie missed one period and waited. The second time she found a doctor who told her she's pregnant. She asked Cleo to call Father Doyle. He'll never let her look for someone who might do an abortion."

"Where is she?"

"Northwestern. The Emergency Room. Cleo took her. Not about being pregnant, but because she had a seizure. She doesn't remember and she's scared, Joe. Her *grand mal* is no longer as controllable. She bit off a corner of her tongue. Not enough to hurt her looks, but she'll know."

"Is it Jeff?"

"That's my guess. Unless you guys know something I don't."

"Has she told him? Whoever it is?"

"My guess is, 'No.' And I wouldn't if I were her. Can you picture Jeff playing house? He's too busy making his end run around Luther for valedictorian *and* class president. Cleo says Frankie wanted you to know."

"Me? I guess I'm flattered. We *have* talked about her reporting for the *Grist*."

"That might help keep her mind off her belly."

"Assuming she stays in school."

"If she conceived in, say April or May, she might finish half of her senior year. If she's not embarrassed to show up and try."

"She's shy."

"And easily scared. You can help. I drove her home after *A Midsummer Night's Dream* and thought something was wrong. Given what our church teaches us, I'm pretty sure she'll go ahead and have the baby. But we can look into adoptions if she wants that. She can't count on much from her parents. I suspect she'd like to keep this secret by going away like Paulette Hawkes did two summers ago."

"What about her cheerleading? Gymnastics? Life?"

"Yeah, all those. No one will notice this spring, but she'll be showing a little by the fourth month and a lot by September, her third trimester if my math's any good."

"Hatch is a severely cold jerk!"

"And he always looks as though he has his act together. Leggy should feel lucky when she realizes she might have been the one waking up with her back on a steel hospital table."[43]

---

[43] MN: Mayhew came over in gym when Hatch, naked, was sweeping papers from his locker onto the wet floor. "You!" Mayhew trumpeted.

"It's Hatch, Sir. Jeff Hatch. You came to one of my tournaments this summer, hit a few balls with my dad."

"So what do you call that stroke?"

"Cleaning, Sir. They should have done this over the summer?"

Mayhew sized up Hatch's tennis legs, loosely knotted forearms, and face that seemed to feint continuously. He also glanced below Hatch's waist. "Are you wising off?"

KN: You told me Jeff was packed.

MN: I hope I said Hatch was a prick. One long royal prick.

Joe hikes east on 50th street from Nicollet, where it rises one block to 1st Avenue before falling in three steep drops to the Parkway and creek, a triple ski jump to Amy's. Melting snow bubbles toward corner drains and moonlight embeds in a low sky. He wants to tell Amy everything, but the news about Frankie does not get a good reaction.

Amy wants to walk up Luverne. The last of the snow remains as icy piles between curbs and sidewalks, packed where children have pretended they were walking mountain trails and leaping crevasses where shoveled sidewalks to the street split the peaks. Amy and Joe walk past twinkling house lights and windows letting in fresh night air.

At the top of Luverne she shows him where, day after day at recess, she and her friends used stones to scratch their initials deep into the school wall. She locates hers and Leggy's and Cleo's. Joe asks, but Amy cannot find Kathy's. He takes off his glove to rub his finger across the grooves created by little girls. He puts a cool finger under the hair on Amy's neck, but she doesn't seem to notice.

As they track down through the slush she finally says, "You probably wish it was *you* and Frankie."

"Oh, come on! How could I possibly wish that?" His gut screams and he wants to sob. "With anyone but you? I haven't even gone out with anyone else."

Suddenly Amy seems remote—in another place, in another season. She takes out her house key, turns away, and closes the door. He doesn't know what, but senses that something has gone terribly wrong with their understanding.

∽

KN: Name the worst discrimination we grew up with in our melting pot of Swedes and Norwegians—Johnsons and Petersons and Andersons—and Germans, until they had to go underground during World War II to find the Jews already there.

MN: Is that a question that you personally want to ask?

KN: Of course! Although true too, it's on the JO list of required early '50s material we're shoehorning in.

MN: Okay then, farmers! Us city kids called them "Hicks!" City vs. Country! *Not* a good-natured rivalry. Also our parents hated, or were scared to death of, liberal radicals: what Minnesota called the Democratic-Farmer-Labor Party. Think Humphrey when he was mayor of Minneapolis and later McCarthy and McGovern. Our folks worshipped multiple-choice presidential candidate Harold Stassen. And Walter Judd, missionary buddy and supporter of Chiang Kai-shek who ripped off most of China with the help of his charming wife, the Madam.

KN: Appearance mattered most!

MN: When they held the State Basketball Tournament in Williams Arena, 32 districts played off to send teams from eight geographic regions.

KN: Stand by Young Quinlan's at the corner of 9th and Nicollet and you couldn't miss the Region 8 timber giants from empty northwest towns like Warroad, Roseau, or the coldest spot in the country, International Falls where Gopher All-American and pro player Bronko Nagurski ran a gas station. Once they'd closed the open-pit mines Region 7's guys from what was once Hibbing's "Million Dollar" High School came to town looking as empty as their mines.

MN: I hated the blonde doctor and meatpacker sons from the southeast who moved like racehorses and sported brand-new silk sweat suits, with tops *and* bottoms.

KN: Don't forget that Leslie Caron, *A Parisian in America*, actually danced to Austin to marry the son of the Hormel canning family. And Rochester! The Clinic, St. Mary's, the estates of Mayowood; hard to find any homeless there.

MN: Picture the western farmers from towns so far away their car radiators boiled over or some small part like a clutch fell off so they arrived late for the tip-off, heads so razor-shaved you'd see bumps—although everyone loved the year little Lynn almost won wearing baggy brown uniforms sewed by their mothers. And one year Canby brought every boy in school: five starters and one substitute to sit on the bench, to take the court only in case of disaster like a starter fouling out.

KN: "Appearance" meant clothes and haircuts. Unexpectedly television performed one national service: it created a "Universal Dress Code": jeans and sneakers, honored from Harlem to Hawaii—although that and Alaska weren't even states when we were growing up. Forty-eight stars on our flag!

MN: And in our days only the farmers wore the jeans, and often bib overalls, which only went main-stream—seen with the eclectic war surplus and beeds costumes of the late '60s and '70s. We got stuffed like sausage into corduroy knickers with long socks until we graduated to corduroy pants, usually in drab green or gray—never with wide wales.

KN: It would be nice to say we had early insights into equality, but we hardly saw a Black or an Hispanic, except the Grahams and Art Robbins, until TV. No one could explain how the school board brought in Kumalo's father Jerome Graham as the city's first Black Superintendant. We were a state full of Native-Americans, referred to as "Indians," but we only let them fascinate tourists by selling toy birch bark canoes in front of teepees that made those driving north for a few weeks in a lake cabin

SPRING '53 • 109

squirm with images of dirt and disease.

MN: Imagine the reaction at Interlachen Golf Club if Joe tried to sign up Leggy for a tee time on a Saturday morning or Wednesday afternoon.

KN: They'd pull him into the caddyshack and spank his bare behind.

MN: So name the *best* of the early '50s. What about that phrase "solid Midwest values" you always toss around but never spell out on our grocery list?

KN: Oh, they were there! Pass the plate of bread, please.

MN: I beg your pardon.

KN: When someone passes you the plate, take the top piece—always. It may be a heel but you don't flip the stack to try for a fresher piece farther down.

MN: And?

KN: When someone says, "Who'll help unload the truck?" you whip up your hand and head over to help out.

MN: But the auto tire ad in *Saturday Evening Post* always said, "Know Competition and You'll Know America!"

KN: A grain of salt, please.

MN: Huh? Oh, I get it. You want us to be flabby patsies? Better red than dead?

KN: Well-read would be good. Check out the big history book and you don't see one gang, like Stalin and friends, taking over the world, do you?

MN: I did hear Eva Braun wouldn't put out for Hitler when he started slipping.

KN: Cultivate your own garden.

MN: That one went by me.

KN: Voltaire! His Candide was a simpleton but you'd find his story puzzling.

MN: Mom didn't teach you all this radical talk.

KN: Nor Mother Church. And hardly the Girl Scouts. But I'd chalk up a bunch of moral influence points for the YW- and YMCA. My single summer at Y Camp—not private Lake Hubert with the other FEMS. And Grade Y at Page, Junior Hi-Y at Ramsey, and Hi-Y and Blue Tri at Washburn: pretty powerful stuff. Those folks coming back from WWII gave us incredible role models. Read Tom Brokaw. He admired the generation coming back from the war more than any other, even though he admitted it was not free of bigotry. But there were tremblings of tolerance. Beginnings that would explode in the '60s, a decade after Joe's Journal and JO's pages.

MN: Was it racist that we laughed at Jack Benny?

KN: Funny, funny man! We pretty much covered the bases with white ethnic radio shows: "The Life of Riley," "Duffy's Tavern," along with Molly Goldberg, George Jessel, Henny Youngman, George and Gracie. Remember José Imenez on the Sullivan show? Or "I Love Luigi"—he was our show-biz "Jolting Joe DiMaggio"—*sans* Marilyn. Unfortunately we also listened to those two white guys Amos and Andy making a living making fun of Blacks.

MN: I picture President-elect Eisenhower meeting with Truman in '52 saying, "Nice move on McArthur, but did you have to integrate the military?"

KN: We went to classes and *lived* in a class system. Still do! Profiteers rose early to rally votes to build clauses into the Constitution that allow them to kick ass continually. Those who help the most get hurt the most. As for artists and "contemplative activists," we get too absorbed to notice the big heel suspended above us. You try to be nice, then nicer, but then wham. Down it comes. Splat!

MN: No, please don't take us back to those days when you'd close in on the bathroom mirror and go pop with your ripest pimple. Enough squabbling!

KN: This isn't squabbling. It's politics.

MN: And how much preaching was JO and how much was you?[44]

---

[44] KN: A thought! For all his niceness, how many times does Joe's Journal mention one of the guys or girls—who took morning classes then went off to a real job? The forgotten Work-Study Students?

MN: I wonder whether Joe knew any. Tell me: would you have dated one?

~

Kathy calls, "Everybody, take ten." She's blocked the opening number with the Greek chorus behind Joe Taylor's mother in bed waiting to give birth. "Look, guys, loosen up. Stop worrying about looking foolish. I'm not."

Hatch, who has the best voice in school, sings Joe's father. He pays no attention when Frankie Hill pushes off the stage and puts her feet up on an auditorium seat next to Joe. She hasn't missed a rehearsal, knows her part, and teaches steps to the other dancers. But just in case, Cleo is learning Frankie's solo.

Kathy talks with Kumalo Graham about creating projections to flash on screens behind the actors. "Good or bad, this has to be special. How many school newspaper staffs put on an original musical? We'll either get an audience like R & H got for their last afternoon run-through—all cheers and crying—or we'll get what they got at their preview the same night: an audience sitting on its hands. I shouldn't tell you, but Hammerstein replaced Agnes de Mille before the opening, the first woman director of a musical in Broadway history. But I'm staying here!"

Frankie looks fine and hasn't told anyone else. Joe pats her knee. "Nice moves. They're going to love you." Frankie's shirt hangs over her shorts. She tells Joe she's started her second trimester and might start showing in another month, but *after* the show. "I won't start my third trimester until October. "It's like semesters," she tries to joke.

"If you can stay in school until the Christmas holidays you might miss only part of one semester."

"I kinda doubt I'll come back. I might join a circus. Learn to walk a wire."

"You've already done that."

Frankie smiles for an instant, then skips to the edge of the stage and points at a cardboard box shaped into a scenery piece. "Do we really want the audience to read that?"

Kathy howls, "Get some paint!"

Leggy turns the box so the audience can no longer read "KOTEX."

Frankie laughs and climbs back onstage. Kathy limps up the side steps.

Summer '53

Summer sunset spreads along the bluff, as the Chevy crawls above the Minnesota River. Amy rotates her wrist so black and gray scarabs catch the orangish rays. Her hands fall to the lap of her white dress, bouncy over layers of petticoat like a petite bale of cotton belted in black. Her fingers check her silver earrings and rub a milky cabochon hanging over her tanned throat.

Rather than turning into the half-moon drive of the Auto Club Chalet, Joe parks in the lot across at the Minnesota Valley Golf Club. He says, "I thought we should settle this before we do any dancing."

"What's to settle now?"

"Our 'Understanding.' College. Our futures."

"You're mad because I didn't wear the new bracelet aren't you?"

"I'm not mad."

"I'll hardly ever take it off, but you don't wear gold with black and white and silver." She taps a pump on the mat. "I want to be a movie: all black and white. So movie me."[45]

---

45. KN: If she wanted to be all black and white and gray like a movie, paint me green. And please don't include another scene like this to show how close they came. Even if he does make what's going to happen quite "suggestive," all right, "damn clear" in his Journal.

They cross the road where headlights flash across her dress. She doesn't wobble but hangs on his arm, tipping slightly, stepping around potholes. As they circle the front canopy, he suggests, "Let's do the gardens first. We need to work all this out."

They pass the Chalet, where candle lamps illuminate star-like corners. They walk where dishes clatter and kitchen voices express relief at another meal's end. The Chalet's hexagonal walls crowned by green-slated gables open to paths curling through clipped and moistened gardens surrounded by white lattice fences.

They pass sheds housing shadowy tractors, mowers, scythes, stacks of clay pots, bags of lime, bales of mulching hay. They unlatch the white gate to the formal gardens and look from the bluff over the river. Trumpets and saxophones float through the screens, pursued by bass and drum. Melodies pass too quickly to name. George M. Cohan gives way to Stephen Foster. Broadway to Camptown. Regards given, ladies singing. Remember me and do-da, do-da. Dixie, dilly-dilly, land of cotton. Black bottoms, lavender blues, and blue rooms. They stand alone under too vast a sky, its oranges and blues extinguishing the few lamps in the river towns below. They straddle the last heights before mid-state Minnesota drops to Iowa and on to the Gulf.

She stretches, scarabs rattling. "If you can lift me up where it's all pink and perfect I might consider not going to Carleton."

"You know you'd like the U."

"I know you can't lift me that high."

The music stops; hands clap; doors bang; voices hum through the shrubbery and bustle toward them. He stands by a gate, picturing her raising a veil and taking someone else's arm.

"You're still mad aren't you?" she asks. "You don't want me to go away but you won't come with me."

"How can I be mad? Crazy maybe."

"Mad under the moon?"

"Let's drive back. Otherwise we won't have enough time."

"Time for I-know-what. Okay! No dances for Amy. And you're the one who says we spend too much time 'making out.' Or for—as I like to call it even though we don't go all the way—'making love.'"

In the car Joe says, "Mickey gave you a compliment."

"A homemade vulgarity, I assume."

"Of course. He says you've got 'one great little rack.'"

"You can't even tell since Dior's 'New Look' gave us back all the cloth they took away during the war. Mickey probably spies when I try on swimsuits or underwear at Dayton's."[46]

"Blue Tango" plays again, then "Old Smoky" and "April in Portugal." Something about Sherman Adams and Seoul. Gertrude Lawrence says hello to young lovers now that she's lost hers and Pat Boone explains that April love is for the very young.

They reach the top of the hill at Luverne and coast, parking behind Rosemary Frayne's bulky pine. Amy belly flops from front to back seat, the white layers of her rear rubbing the ceiling. Stations crackle as Joe moves the dial so Patti Page can croon while he pats Amy's behind.

"Stop! You'll break something."

"Nothing there to break."

She flips, wiggling to reach his hands. He bumps his head climbing to the backseat where his legs hang into the well, hers fitting along the upholstery. They meet facing sideways. Her breath swells like a swimmer's as Patti gives way to Helen O'Connell.

Amy unhooks the black belt and unbuttons. She shrugs off her dress and kicks off crinolines until she's left only in a half-slip and stockings. She raises her arms to the ceiling. "See! I don't alway's need a bra."

[46.] MN: Can we slow down now that we're getting to the part where she's going to take off her dress?

She lays the dress across the front seat, unclipping her earrings with two snaps. She pushes the half-slip down, leaving only nylon over the girdle holding up her stockings.

A streetlight crescent highlights her face. Her shoulders shine as she scratches where her dress was. He enfolds the hand she holds over what she calls "my smaller one."

"A blossom!" he says.

"Blossoms fall." She kicks her pumps off and tucks her legs under. Her shiny knees point right at him. Through the needles of Rosemary's pine they see a light still on in her living room.

"What if a car stops?" he asks.

"You'll hand me your coat and smile a whole lot."

The night sky drains, leaving them slipping toward lighter grays. They slosh and arch in cramping comfort. They thrash. They touch and retouch.

His fingers play across her silky front.

"Save me! I'm helpless—flat on my back. I think I'm pretty bare."

He smoothes her from ankles over knees to the roundness of her rear. "You're not wearing those part-way stockings are you? You don't have bare knees."

"Bernese are big mountains and I wore long stockings tonight so I wouldn't catch cold. Leave them on."

He strokes up and down where her legs widen, fingers gliding across the smooth span from her stocking tops to the looser elastic and tighter girdle edge.

"Okay, you might as well take them off. No, not my stockings! They're not in the way."

She helps pull, separating her legs so the back of his hand brushes over her. "It's springy," he says.

"My favorite season."

"This is really you?"

"This is me. Not much more me to see. I'm about as wide open as a girl can get wearing a girdle. Now you know why we wear panties on the outside. See how nicely they came off? Of course if you're in a real rush—like if you have to pee

—do this." She presses her hands to her hips and slides everything from her hips to below her knees, twisting to free her feet. "Hey, don't put a runner in my stockings. Young Quinlan's finest: 'Size A Nude.' Aren't you proud to be here to protect them?"

"We should slow a little, shouldn't we?"

"We should stop a little, maybe."

"Trouble is: the later it gets, the less time we have."

"Well fella, I don't see you lying there without clothes."

He undresses down to his shorts, all the time kissing and hugging and trying to keep his hand over her bareness. "You're so ...soft."

"Am I supposed to say, 'You're so hard'?"

"I wish I could see better. I know you're darker here, but are you sorta blonde? Like your head?"

"My head is not blonde. It's lemon-straw. You told me that. It's not unusual to be lighter one place and darker another. Check out the eyebrows. That's the best test—sometimes."

"I fell in love when I saw you wet. At Carrie's. Actually I fell in love the first week of homeroom."

"I had my period that night skinny dipping. I don't tonight."

He pushes so her back fits the hollow of the seat and *he* fits *her*. They wrap arms and hold on even when they begin to tingle and go numb. They almost forget to breathe. Neither notices that the light in her living room has been turned off.

"I don't think we're...going to make babies, are we?" Joe asks.

"I believe you'd know if we were."

"I wouldn't want you to have a baby if you didn't want to."

"Not too likely, Chester. Not while you've got those shorts on. Take 'em off."

"Do you mean it?"

"Duh? No, I meant.... They don't make any difference. I forgot about boys having a fly in front of their shorts. You may have noticed, girls don't."

He slips them off, so they join the pile on the floor. "I guess we only have a few more minutes. We can't come in when it's getting light like we did last time. And it's awful if your mother is sitting at the kitchen table waiting."

"Huggies first," she says. "And take everything very very slowly."

Their bodies, bare for the first time above and below the waist, pull tighter. He drops a hand from the curves above to the spaces below. He covers her with his palm and feels how naturally a finger slides in. When it happens, he realizes she must have let him. She must feel it! A breeze blows. Dew hits their backs with a hot dampness.

"That tickles," she says. "I don't think it's supposed to. No, wait! It's not tickling now." She lies farther back and wraps her hand around him. At first only holding on.

"That feels unbelievable," he groans.

"That feels so good too, but too many touches and the phone by daddy's bed will ring."

The slower he moves his finger inside her the faster she moves her hand up and down on him. He feels drawn into velvet, helped by her rocking hips. He wonders about the barrier everyone mentions. Maybe he should have reached it. Unless as everyone jokes, she used to ride horses or slide down banisters.

After his finger seems to have sunk as far as it can, and he has settled into a rhythmic in-and-out glide, she moans and grabs him by the shoulders. She shudders but keeps her hand moving on him.

Instinctively he drops his face and feels a tickle and smells lavender. Her hips rock until she shudders again, hanging on with her legs as she cries out.

Their chins connect and he hears himself echoing, "I love you. I love you. So much."

When car lights approach, they crush each other. When the lights pass, they wait. Finally she says, "We better go in."

"Sure," he says. Neither moves. He puts his hand over where she holds him and points himself to where she's so open.

"No!" she says.

"No?" He touches his tip to her and lets himself trail down until he can't be sure whether he's reached her hair.

"Not here!"

He pulls back, suspending himself above her. "No?"

"Not here!"

"Not here?" He's afraid he's going to explode.

She cradles his head and opens her mouth around his, wrapping her legs so when he does explode the wetness lands mostly on her belly, some on her hairs.

They lie still until she touches between them. She gives him a long liquid kiss. He squeezes and pulls her to him, each feeling the stickiness they have created together.

Then stockingless, she slips into her heels and gathers her clothes. The car smells wonderfully of silky Tabu wisps and scents they have released for the first time.

She looks so calm. No one could tell how close they've come.[47]

---

[47] MN: Our boy finger fucked her for God's sake! And almost slid into home base.

KN: Mickey!

MN: I'm about as technically correct as you can get. Do you want names for all the body parts and the rest of what they did, and what we must assume they did other nights?

KN: If anyone was, is, and will always be the quintessence of what we call "sophomoric," step forward. Michael, the prize goes to you.

MN: "Quintessence"? Is that what Miss Marsh made Joe write that English paper about?

Mickey takes the bike he finds leaning by the front glass of Dix's Drug Store at 48th and Nicollet. He pedals south past Ramsey, dipping down hills toward the Parkway through Tangletown. His legs give out as he reaches the mid-point of another hill.

Walking the bike deliberately, he sees her lying on a beach towel in her side lawn. He isn't sure he dares stop and imagines if he calls out that his voice will echo as far as the Washburn Water Tower, with its eight hooded sword-carrying flanking figures brooding down from its hilly peak.

As he walks the bike by, she sits up. It's not Frankie. It's her little sister. She waves. He waves back and keeps his wheels moving until he can climb on and coast down another hill.[48]

---

[48] KN: Oh I don't doubt you liberated the bike, but I never saw this scene in the Journal.

MN: I call this one of them artistic licenses. It *did* happen, whether Joe knew about it or not.

～⃥

Amy rocks in a hammock balancing a glass and pitcher of iced tea. Joe sits next to her on the Johnson side lawn. He says, "So we've graduated. Doesn't exactly feel like a rocket going off. Actually I miss it already."

"The summer's going grand."

"And I'm going to miss you more than it."

"So why join the millions crossing the Mississippi to lose themselves at the U. Come to Carleton. They'd accept you in a minute. Yale and Princeton did."

"Dinky nine-hole course, small theater, and it's not Minneapolis. I want what we've had."

"If you come to Carleton we can study a little and hold hands for four years. It's a great college in a neat little town where Jesse James robs banks. We'd be less than an hour from here and I can keep daddy and mummy away, except Parents' Weekend and Homecoming. I'm not asking you to go to St. Olaf. Come with me and they'll call you a "Carlie," not a 'Hairy Oley.'"

"Kathy's still pushing the East. Now Princeton more than Yale. She talks about the Triangle Club and its original musicals that get on the Ed Sullivan Show. Minnesota's football team would beat them bad, although that fellow Kazmaier we've watched on TV looks pretty good."[49]

"Too bad you can't give one of your scholarships to Kathy. She's the one who'd get the most out of it. She can't afford any place but the U."

"The U's a damn good university."

"But Carleton's a place where a father, or an intimate friend, can trust that their daughter, or that intimate friend's friend, will remain protected while getting a good education."

[49.] KN: The Triangle Club *was* and *is* a big deal, founded in 1893 by Booth Tarkington. F. Scott Fitzgerald, Jimmy Stewart, Jose Ferrer, Myron McCormick, Joshua Logan, *You're a Good Man Charlie Brown's* Clark Gesner, *Blue Lagoon's* Brooke Shields, and Washburn's Joe Taylor performed in and wrote its shows.

"They don't have boys down there?"

"Of course they do. Better come along so you won't have to worry."

They sit for the thousandth time on the Nolan front steps.

"You *must* change your mind," Kathy tells Joe. "It's what you *need*. Think of it! A scholarship for half of the tuition: $1,000. It's the East. I'd take it in a snap. Stay here like me and what do you get? Same crowd, same movies, same burger joints. Lots of parties. Not tame like ours have been either. College isn't that way. You should hear Woody Chesney's college war stories. You'll waste time at Dinkytown, where they sell 3.2 beer with free popcorn. Even Carleton would be more of an adventure. Don't you want adventures?"

"I've always wanted to go to the U. I didn't let Amy talk me into Carleton, and we've been close for more than two years."

Kathy gives her corduroy cuffs two rolls. "*We've* been close for more than a dozen."

"You're probably right. I suppose you *are* right. You always have been right."

Sitting on top of one of the high stone ticket booths across from their houses Mickey says, "Yeah, I'd say it's time to dump her. At college you'll be dropped into a bowl with so many cunts and tits you won't know which way to lick first. What more can you do with Amy?"

"I'm not sure," Joe says. "She's always talked about college weekends, here or down in Northfield. That doesn't sound bad. I'm kind of fuzzy about what's beyond this summer."

"Wait till she's gone and write a letter. All the guys do that. I would if I were going to college and had someone to write. Maybe you can come up with an address of some broad who's about to be kissed off and I can write her—if Kathy will help me."

"I'm not kissing her off. I'm just unsure about all the newness. How can anything be better than these last years—with her?"

"Listen up: I've got some nifty phrases. Write 'em down before I forget 'em."

"I'm not sure...."

"Who says you have to be. Write 'em down. You can decide after you get to Princeton whether or not to mail the letter.

〜

After dancing the cobblestones of Copenhagen with Danny Kaye and Jeanmarie at the Parkway Theater, Amy looks as though she isn't going to cross the creek.

Joe says, "You're frosted because you drove by when Kathy and I were talking on her steps. She's not getting to go East and she's so much smarter than her marks or scores show. She's fun. She's fast."[50]

Amy sits on a rock, wrapping her arms around her knees. Light rain falls, beats tapping from trees to the trickle of creek. "Why couldn't we have picked the same college? Carleton would have been perfect."

"I thought you wanted me to go to Princeton. And there's something else. What if you meet someone else? What if, sooner or later, he tries to touch you. When I touched you… that was your first time, right?"

"Yes."

"You acted as though it was so natural."

"Yes."

"Well I don't want anyone else to touch you."

"I don't *want* anyone else to touch me."

"No touching! And I'd hate to hear you'd started to smoke. Those gotta stay parts of our understanding."

"It's getting bigger. Our understanding, I mean."

"Will you do it? I mean not do it?"

"Why wouldn't I?"

"I worry what college might do to us. You're perfect right now. I can't stand the idea of anyone but me putting anything in your mouth or…."

"I get the idea."

"I love you."

---

50. KN: "Fast"? Thanks a heap, Joe-boy. That's exactly what all girls want to be. You saw me climb the fence. Do you want to see me round the curve and knock over a few low hurdles? "Fun": that's an okay thing to be. I better take that, and run—fast!

She looks so close to saying the words, but doesn't. Instead she hugs and kisses him until he thinks he knows what her silence means.

They don't talk "engagement" or "marriage" but each assumes they are sliding toward those. However Kathy says, "No! You don't *slide*. You consider and plan. You *choose*! And hope you've chosen correctly. Some people even do."

Mist rises from sidewalks. Streetlights shimmer in puddles. The air moves so slowly they can bite the scents of late summer. Barefoot, Amy slaps the pavement, puddle-splashing her legs. She reaches up under her thin skirt to tug her blouse below her waist.

They step across the rocks and climb from the creek bed to the bridge where the Parkway drops from Joe's home to hers. He holds her against one of the sandstone pylons to shield her from headlights. "Duck! If we start saying goodbye here we'll never get home early like we said we would."

"I can *hear*. Accidents happen to children and drunks. I'm neither. Let's sit."

They walk on to the wall at the foot of her alley, sitting and leaning against the shrubbery that always scratches their backs. She finds a stick and bangs the postal storage box. "Less than a quarter full. They'll pick up at noon. As soon as your train moves, write. Here's where they'll store it for me. I'll write back and promise not to tell you more about Petra Malcolm."

"And her heavy cramps?"

"She actually went to a doctor to be fitted. Rosemary says men prefer that way."

"Rosemary-Next-Door gets all the hot bulletins, doesn't she?"

"A woman cannot ignore protection."

They turn up her alley, passing garages, fenced garbage cans, barking dogs. Kitchen lights look hazy behind curtains, rosy and translucent. Their arms automatically wrap each other's waists and she hooks a thumb under his belt, pulling him along by the hips as the incline increases.

"Here's where you got grease on your shorts. And all cut up."

"I'm not wearing shorts. We call this a 'skirt.'"

Her perfume competes through the mist with leaf smoke. Crisp browns, oranges, and yellows blow down her alley, reminding him of a pile raked high enough to jump in and the smell of grass stain from knee football.

He moves her thumb and puts his arms around her. He feels her nose on his throat, her chin pressed into his breastbone. He runs his hands over her blouse as she edges to the high side of the alley to bring her mouth level with his.

He wants to shout, "Not being together tomorrow. It can't be!"

They walk until they see the light at her kitchen table. They stand by her single-car garage and tool shed and garden fence. She whispers, "You haven't, but you should. I mean: ask what I want, Dumbo! As a coming home present at Christmas. A girl has wants. Start with a postcard. No, daddy, can read that. Make it a cottage. Maybe by a waterfall. With tea for several. And at least one bluish room and a greenery. Better make it a cottage for two."

"How about paper dolls? Jim Stewart, Vic Mature, all Three Stooges?"

"I'd prefer furniture. Not much at first. And a black wool sweater like the sailors wear at Minnetonka and White Bear."

"Little-girl size?"

"With china and silver—a few pieces. You can help pick the pattern."

"Do you know how old we are?"

"Seventeen and one-half and eighteen, and when we graduate from college we'll be older."

"There's so much I've got to do. I want to do well in school, and be in shows, write songs, get elected to things."

"Why?"

"That's the way it's done. Don't you want to?"

"Get elected? Why would I? What would anyone want to elect me to? I told you, we don't have to buy everything now.

I'm only telling you what I'd like. It's 'Amy's Wish List.' Why not be prepared with china and silver patterns? I'm not asking for a baby yet."

"Don't do that to me! We can't have...anything from what we've done so far, I don't think. Can we?"

"Ph-e-e-r!" She holds out a limp wrist.

"The last few times we've come pretty close."

"Da-ah!" Her wrist goes limp again. "Gracious! You're such a worry."

"In the car in front of your house?"

"I've gotten my period since then. So there!"

"When?"

"Oh, a couple of weeks ago." She pats below his belt. "Is this something you want to worry about?"

They hug, her skirt catching a shed board and riding up. She doesn't tug it down as his mouth muffles hers. "I told my folks I wouldn't let you walk home late. Your train leaves so early." Her hand moves between them.

He drifts, keeping the kitchen lamp in sight. "You're making it hard. No joke."

"No kidding. Now that you've got this, I can't let you say goodbye to mummy and daddy."

"Can you imagine how I feel leaving? Doesn't that tear you apart? I've said, 'I love you'—lots."

"And I've said I find it easier to write than say it. Besides I have told you, sort of...."

"Sorta in whispers and pants."

"Not in pants. I'm not wearing any."

"Under your skirt?"

"Well I am, but they're too thin to count. So's my skirt."

He touches her, feeling the slide of silk on nylon. She looks up at him. Her lashes blink. Her eyes water.

"Your face is wet. You *are* tearing."

"We're standing in rain."

She sobs, shaking and shrinking, sinking back into the shed's clapboards. She backs inside. He brushes cobwebs from her face as she pushes aside a bag of fertilizer, a spade, a spreader. She brings his hand beneath the window to the sharp edge of a license plate nailed to the wall. "Feel this: the secret hiding place for all my valuables. Right now, paper plates and plastic spoons; when I come back from Dayton's, silver and china."

"Please don't do that to me!"

"We *must* leave messages." She plucks an imaginary pen from the air. "There! A list of everything we'll need at first. We'll keep the list behind the license and add as we think of things. You can come here on vacations."

Back in the wet air they cling under the shed's overhang. He cannot see the kitchen when he presses her into the wall.

"Very nice," she says. "I think you pushed me into wet paint."

"That's only 'rain.'"

"It could be paint powder. Want to feel?"

He touches round her rear and hips, staying away from her front.

"You didn't get it all."

Hands roam. Breathe blends. Unsteady legs bend. She presses a bare heel into the shed. Thin layers slide against each other. His throat goes dry as bones bump and hips hurry, rotating, softly slamming, her nylon blending into his cotton, she moving faster. His muscles tighten while she wraps her legs and keeps squeezing.

She drops a hand between them and brings away some of the wetness. He says, "I think the mist got thicker. Went right through our clothes."

Head back she starts moving again, feeling his renewed stroking until she rises and falls in relieving spasms.

She pokes his ribs. "God, that feels so heavenly! Does anyone else know that?"

"Only us. We're alone. Together. But I wonder what can soak through what?"

"Four layers? Sorta thin, but probably no need to worry. Although 'two weeks after' is not exactly a safe time. Does that scare you?"

"How do they expect you to remember in the middle of…when you're feeling like that?"

"I didn't. But as Rosemary would say, "Even when you're trying, the odds are against you most days of the month."

"Terrific!" Joe drops his hands and wipes them on his sides.

"No," Amy says, "You definitely don't look ready for cribbage with daddy. Now I'm going to have to wait outside till they go to bed."

"I'll wait with you."

"No, you go. You've got to travel. If I go in now it'll either be 'bad Amy who's late again' or 'bad Amy who's got a guy's gunk on her.' I prefer to wait until they're in bed."

The kitchen light goes out. Joe asks, "Do you think it can get up in you before it dries?"

"You mean if my hand got a real sperm on it and that hand got too close? Or weren't there any real sperm mixed in with the other stuff?"

"Big joke! They say it only takes one."

"And they say it doesn't matter if you're standing up, having the curse, doing it the first time, or putting it in and taking it out before the stuff comes out."

"We weren't doing any of those—except standing."

"Petra and Noah had a real scare when he got close. For most of a month, they pictured an upstream swimmer and he didn't even put it in."

"Having a baby and not even…?"

"You don't have to draw a picture. But then we could get married and do it all the time."

"Yeah."

He guides her past her father's strong, sweet roses. At the side door he pulls her blouse out of her skirt and lowers it as far over her hips as it will fall.

"Remember! Write, right away, and buy me things. And don't worry. I'll write and let you know if anything happens."

"Am I supposed to look forward to that?"

"Anything like if I get a simply great history professor or a roommate with fantastic clothes. Anything like that! Or if you're worried about the other stuff and you want me to write when something happens—say in a couple of weeks— I will. Because it *will* happen. Don't worry"

She holds the screen while he turns the key. His mouth aims and misses, smearing her already blurred beauty spot.

Fall '53

Four Princeton roommates spend Saturday fixing their suite: two bedrooms off a sitting room with a fireplace and casement windows opening from Blair Tower toward Lockhart and Henry Hall Courtyards. From there it's the eastern flatlands an hour to the Atlantic.

"Go ahead and mail it," the roommate from New Trier says. "It sounds right to me."

The one from Woodbury-Forest, which he keeps calling "the Groton of the South," says, "Agreed! No one goes ape over old high school girlfriends—except wonks and weenies."

"Millions of dollies to meet," the boy says, who spent an extra "PG" year prepping down the road at Lawrenceville. "You're in fat city. You don't want to commit now."

"Why pick one girl?" Ed from New Trier High says. "We don't even pick a major till sophomore spring." With Ed and Joe the suite splits fifty-fifty between public and private school graduates, exactly the split in the college, the first year the privates have not dominated since Princeton's founding as the College of New Jersey in 1746.

"I just want to get through this," Joe says. "All those assignments already posted in the entries of McCosh and Dickinson and we haven't been to our first class. No marks until midterms and everything riding on finals in January. I don't even know where I'll be in January."

"I think this epistle provides a splendid text for your purpose," the Woodbury-Forest man declares. "You have a bit of a way with words."

"I got some help with the letter."[51]

"Getting help is not exactly in the spirit of Princeton's Honor System," the Lawrenceville PG says. "I ought to know."

"That's only for exams and course papers, Yankee."

"So what are you going to do?" Ed asks.

"I think I should wait. Give it till Monday at least. We expected to be only an hour away: the University of Minnesota and Carleton."

"Carleton's very shoe," Woodbury-Forest says. "Iowa?"

"That's Grinnell," Ed says.

"But she's not there," Joe says. "When I changed from Minnesota to here she got her dad to send her East to Smith. That makes a difference in how I feel: kinda chased."

"Here's a swift ploy," says Woodbury-Forest. "Go up to the Hamp for a weekend, hang your tie on her house door, bang her a few times, eat breakfast there so she can score points with her friends. Come back, then send the letter to Northampton."

"Gross!" the Lawrenceville guy says.

"Let's hike to Murray-Dodge for some coffee," Ed suggests. "Maybe you'll decide to mail your pronouncement on the way back. I've got to put in another couple of hours in the Libe. I'm already clutched about my courses."

"Are we supposed to be reading already?" Joe asks. "There's no one here to ask."

"Welcome to college. Almost the real world. Of course not the South. How would you guys feel about a rebel flag over the fireplace?"

---

51. KN: Letter?
MN: Hold your water! Patience is virtuous. You must have left the room when I set that chapter of the Journal aside.

In a Freshman Week exchange of letters Kathy has written, "Fess up. You're pissed that Amy's tagging along, aren't you? Well I think you should be." When he wrote back, Joe wasn't sure what to say but he didn't mention the remarkably literate letter that Mickey had given him.[52]

He *is* pissed that Amy's followed him and writes everyday. He's also pissed that she's now writing, "I love you"—over and over again as though her needle got stuck in a groove.

[52] KN: Okay, I remember my letter about "Amy tagging along," but what's this "remarkably literate letter" you gave him?

Joe has no plan to meet her in New York City but his buddy Ed herds him into the shuttle to Grand Central. "It's the starting point: 'Under the clock at the Biltmore' is *the* place on Thanksgiving weekend. You might wangle an introduction to Frank Costello during a recess of the Crime Commission."

Bumped, Joe mistakenly steps into the revolving door with an older guy and his crimson and white scarf, striped umbrella, and crimson-patterned tie. The guy glares as they revolve to the foot of the grand stairs. Joe looks up the stairs where a crown of curled and polished wood hangs out from the wall to frame an oval clock.

Under the clock he faces a flower-framed patio with a piano, where friends lean in to talk to those with tables. To the left, elevator doors open to deposit descending bouquets, replacing them immediately with ascending ones. Girls enter the lobby as though they have walked straight from their baths, hair satin and velvet like their gowns. Faces shine around ivory smiles; thick lipsticks spread in holiday shades. A girl with bangs taps a friend. A silver flare snaps and a charcoal arm lowers a flame to light the cigarette between her lips.

To his right, boys hang off wall phones. Others wait. Joe walks past cages where clerks check reservations, while a conga line like the sailors leading Rosalind Russell at the Winter Garden weaves by.

On the carpet by potted palms and carelessly piled overcoats Joe stamps out a cigar and waits for a phone. A high humming hurts his ears, as do rhythmless chatter and booming desk bell pings. He inhales what he guesses is rum and knows is dead tobacco, spearmint and dirty carpet. He can make no sense of one girl's hand and eye signals.

When a phone is free he asks for "Miss Johnson," almost hanging up before a voice drawls, "She's ironing, but I might fetch her if you'll presume to tell me who might be calling."

He has a second chance to hang up but says, "Tell her it's a friend. A friend from high school."

"You *are* a tease. That's simply charming. You hang on now, hear? I'll run see whether she might be available."

Amy's voice sounds flat. "Is that you?"

"I'm downstairs. Who was that?"

"I *wrote* you. That's Cynthia Buckley. She's White Bear and Summit. Very rich, right Cindy?"

"She didn't sound like an orphan."

"Her family's in flour. I wrote you'd like her. We're both in the same house."

"Jordan!"

"I'm surprised you remember. It would have been nice if you'd answered my letters. *Before* that one of yours. Look, I'm only wearing a slip and I'm ironing my dress to go out."

"Which dress?"

She leaves him wondering what she might be doing before answering, "You've never seen it."

"Can you come down?"

"You wrote that you didn't want to see me."

He pictures the last draft of the letter, copied from the draft before it. "I didn't exactly say that."

"That's what I read. I'm going to scorch my dress."

"What color?"

"Powder blue. White piping and pleats."

"Why don't you turn off the iron? You must have time to talk. I only said we shouldn't get too serious, too soon. We have so much time."

"Well, I *stopped* being too serious." He hears the phone drop. He waits, wondering whether they are still connected. "You can come up. For a few minutes. But I have to get dressed."

"They won't let me up. Something about boys and girls on odd and even floors."

"Ride to the ninth and walk down one. No, you'll need to show a room key. What are you wearing?"

"The blue suit we graduated in. A scarf-like Scotch tape."

"Cynthia'll be down. Wait by the elevator farthest from the clock. Remember: you can't stay and I can't go out with you."

"Who is he?"

"Only an Amherst."

"My purple and white scarf will be hanging out."

"Stick with Scotch tape, or try purple and tan. Purple and white's Williams."

"Send down the flour heiress. We'll talk some prep."

A strong-legged girl with reddish pigtails pushes from an elevator, making enough space to spread her elbows, cup her hands, and light a cigarette. She exhales as she drawls, "You're Joe? You've been bad and now you're going to be good." She measures him from one blue-padded shoulder to the other, grabbing his scarf to lead him toward an elevator. She presses a key into his palm. "That's Lester Lanin's main band in there. Lester himself. Flash the key, but don't let them see the number."

She's made her quick entrance and exit. He holds up the key and rides an all-male elevator to nine.

He spots Cynthia on the stairway motioning him to follow. "Actually they don't care if a boy gets up here unless he and his girlfriend get too drunk and make too much noise when they screw."

Cynthia Buckley leads him to the partly open door of 844. "You can go in long as you're good, but keep both feet on the bed, hear?" She hangs the "Do Not Disturb" sign, grinning as though she knows more about Amy than he does.

Cynthia strides back toward the elevators where Joe pictures her blending with, while adding a new character to, the lobby pageant.

Amy in her slip holds an iron over a light blue silk he has never seen. Both beds need making. Newspapers and ashtrays litter the room. Clothes drip from suitcases. Towels

hang over chairs, underwear over the shower rod. The
bureaus hold packs of Kents and Kools, theatre programs,
deodorant, scattered change and bills.

Amy looks shorter in stockings that wrinkle over ankles
as she presses the steaming weight into the fabric. Her shoulders seem smaller and paler. Her blue-iced slip looks new
but wrinkled.

"I'm going to flunk out before Christmas," she says.

"Everybody thinks that. Even the super-brighties."

"It's harder when you stop studying. Cynthia wrote part
of my last paper. We're not on the Princeton Honor System."

He moves an ashtray from the bed to the bureau, pushing
aside clothes he's never seen. "We could go somewhere. Get
you back in time for your date." The word "date" stabs him.
"I don't know my way around, but there must be someplace
...to talk."

"Why talk? I memorized your letter."

"One letter shouldn't matter much."[53]

"Well I didn't find a P.S. informing me of that. Ask
Cynthia. I got the letter after class, in Jordan, right before
lunch. I remember what I was wearing, the china on the
table—everything! I could count every tear in September, in
October. All the time except when I was asleep."

"I'm sorry."

"Big help! I even called Rosemary and asked her to look
in my secret hiding place under the license plates in case you
mailed a retraction to the wrong address. Rosemary reported
'No messages.'" Amy tips the iron on end and turns the
dress.

"Your friend Cynthia's swift. Where did she get that
Southern sound? And if she plays sports why does she
smoke?"

"She can imitate anyone. She's got you down by now.
Probably got her friends laughing in the lobby. Her family

---

53. KN: Someone's not playing fair. We don't know what this letter actually said.
MN: Blame Joe. I guess he didn't copy it into his Journal.

did Nag's Head before they delivered her to Northampton. She arrived with an accent so good that the Carolina girls took her as native. She doesn't smoke that much, but field hockey's over and she says smoking makes her feel good. She races the Inner Lakes on Minnetonka and wins. She'd probably like you, but she goes with a senator's son who was tapped for St. Anthony's."

"That a big deal?"

"Not everyone at Yale gets into it—or 'Bones' or 'Scroll.'"

"She looks like she's been around boats all her life and never worn a life preserver."

"I've learned a lot from her."

"Why don't you put on that fabulously ironed dress and we'll go out?"

"My blue is for later. Would you promise to get me back in time?" She yanks the cord from the socket, puts on a charcoal skirt, pulls down a light gray sweater, and steps into black heels in a single balletic motion. Obviously Cynthia has taught her to spend less time getting ready. "Stay where you are; I'm going in there first." She closes the bathroom door behind her.

On the street Joe shakes his head when a uniformed man starts to call a cab. Amy's purse hangs off the shoulder of her familiar vanilla coat. Her hair has grown longer, maybe not as yellowish but crowned by the same gold headache band she wore in high school. He says, "New hairstyle?"

She glares. "What's *your* trouble?"

"You look different."

"I *am* different."

He grabs for a wrist, lost in cuffs that used to warm them both. They leave the crush around the hotel and walk two long blocks west, not quite to the theaters, and two short blocks north.

"That's enough," she says. They turn and walk back to the hotel.

Outside the Biltmore's revolving doors he asks, "Can I come up?"

"You *were* up. I'm going right out."

"To do what?"

"We have tickets to a new play: *Save the Jaguar*. It's got a strange kid who's going to do a Steinbeck movie with Julie Harris. He's supposed to be fabulous. Gotta go."[54]

"Look, we could ride the subway. Take the ferry past the Statue to Staten Island." A cab threatens to clip the back of Joe's trousers.

"You can always write, you know." Her face looks as though it might tear up like the last night by her garage. She takes off her headache band, one side of her face partly hidden as she smoothes her hair with her fingers.

"Here!" She hands him the band. "Take it and bring it back tomorrow. No Thanksgiving date so far for Amy! Why don't you stay over or come back?"

He hesitates. She takes back the band.

"I have to study and help build sets. You wouldn't believe how many pages we have in world history alone."[55]

"Invite me to Princeton for a weekend. We have two left before the holidays. Girls pay their way down and we could split the costs of food and a room."

"I'll see."

"And we can meet in Chicago and finish the train ride home. Maybe it'll snow in the Wisconsin hills and we can watch all those little towns go by, lit with Christmas lights."

"Let me see how much work I can get done. If I can't train back to the city tomorrow, I can write you."

"Please don't stay away again. You're here now, but you blow so hot and cold. It's been awful! If not Thanksgiving,

---

[54] MN: I know! That was "our" James Dean—when he was alive—before *East of Eden*. Damn if he didn't pass that slouch down for generations.

[55] KN: God! At the U we had to beg the instructor to look at our papers. Sometimes they showed up to drink at the same parties as students. And some would look over the students to find one to take home.

MN: Never you?

KN: Never me.

meet me in Union Station before Christmas. I'll be coming from the East on the New York Central and you'll ride the Broadway Limited. Try! Now, I've got to go in."

She backs through the revolving doors, looking so pretty and sad he can hardly bear it. He wants her to revolve and spin to the curb rather than stop in the lobby. He knows what "awful" feels like. But a boy and girl twirl Amy from the sidewalk and he watches her climb the red-blanketed stair toward the Biltmore clock.

Christmas '53

"Cynthia!" she announces waving once at Joe and twice at a redcap. "Cynthia Buckley! The Biltmore elevator!"

Joe feels the firm shake and notices red pigtails and strong arms with downy hairs and freckles. He glances around Chicago's domed Union Station to see whether she's alone.

"She—our mutual friend, the Johnson girl—communicated with you I assume. Told you she went home a week early?"

"Actually I didn't know that. Is she all right?"

"Nothing that a few B's, even some C's, wouldn't fix—and a social life. I gather you're not currently coupling?"

"We're sort of back where we were last fall."

Up the train steps, the redcap stays ahead like a Class A caddie. Joe stops by the air-powered doors marked "Men." "Don't bother," she says. "Use mine. That's what it's for. Daddy always gets me a room—even if it's not overnight to St. Paul." Joe has to flatten himself against the wall when someone passes but he stays reasonably close to hips that he pictures delivering a considerable body check.[56]

---

56. KN: Bright, rich jock with a good tailor.

    MN: I got a look at the Buckley broad. Yes, sir. She was racing at Minnetonka. Entertaining in her bikini. I'd say she'd give away 20 pounds to you in the ring, say your 140 to her 120. But I bet she could put any of those sailor boys away as fast as she could put any attacker on their back whether they played on ice or grass or her bed.

    KN: I heard Philya, her younger sister by two years, is faster and ahead in smarts and looks, although I'm sure they'll continue to invite the same dress designers into their modest Summit Avenue mansion.

Cynthia settles in her compartment while he uses her toilet, not able to hold the faucet down hard enough to mask his stream. He knows not to flush in the station, and doesn't, but closes the lid. As soon as he comes out, she goes in.

He sits under the swell of folded bed, by the streaked window facing away from Lake Michigan. Her fur coat hangs on a hook, her two largest suitcases balanced high on the rack, the smaller on the floor. The engine quiets so he can hear the tinkle of her charm bracelet, probably as she wipes herself. He pictures the naked girl on the rock swinging from her wrist. Hans Andersen! He hears Cynthia go ahead and flush.

Returning she says, "Like a racehorse! I've been holding it in since Ohio became Indiana. Or is it Ohio becoming Illinois? Geography's no fun except when they're putting up lots of new flags and moving those little countries around."

The train jerks, slows, and begins to pass miles of switches and towers and tracks. She reads while he watches industrial gloom spreading endlessly north. She makes notes in her Modern Library *Plutarch.*

The engine pulls them toward the suburban towns that rise by the great lake: democratic Evanston, the jewel of Kenilworth, preppy Winnetka and Glencoe, luxurious Highland Park, and the priceless outpost at Lake Forest. A light dusting of snow begins before they pass the Great Lakes Naval Training Station and Waukegan, hometown of Jack Benny.

Waiting under the covered Milwaukee Station, she lights a cigarette, inhaling smoke as thought that were a natural function. She asks him about boys he might know. He asks about Plutarch and she answers in Latin. He asks about sailing and she switches back to English.

Grime coats the ledge under his elbow. Inland, snow starts to cover the farms. As the train crosses Wisconsin the sky darkens, dropping heavier flakes. Cars plow home. Dinners cook. Children play.

"Ever try lacrosse?" she asks. "I figure I'll go out for the freshman team this spring. Or do you think I'll be too out of shape from these?" She lights another, waving her wrist with its Timex on a new white and tan band. "Amherst," she says. "With the world's best watch. I see lacrosse as a thinking person's game, and glorious as ballet," which she pronounces to rhyme with "valley" the way Moira Shearer and Amy do.

Joe cannot imagine her losing at anything. He sees her broad back leaning over a boat beam, butt solidly straddling the deck, one hand loosely tapping the tiller, the other tugging the jib line as she barks orders at her crew. He sees some poor preppy slob exposed on the bow, taking all the cold spray. He sees her fists rise in a victory salute, red underarm wisps plastered to her skin.

"I guess Amy's had a rough term," he says. "Is she okay?"[57]

"She postponed two finals. No she's not okay, and you can't do anything about it unless you really want to."

"Sounds as though she needs big help."

"Yup! Hard to argue she didn't get the royal shaft." Cynthia puts the hand with the white and purple band on his; he puts his on hers. She brings up her other hand laughing, "Wanna play 'work up'? I'll win and get first bats. I could always beat my brothers. I'm one who would never have let you treat me the way you treated Amy. I like her a lot, especially if she'll smile. And you better start worrying how you'll treat other people. You're going to meet a lot of them. Girls, I mean."

"I felt all confused this fall."

"No excuses. My 9th grade sister Philya turned 14, and she can already do everything. She got father to get Meyer Davis

---

57. MN: I saw Amy at Theodore Wirth Chalet that Christmas. She looked awful—for her. Her eyes retreated like raccoons with the flu. Not that I'd take my hands off her tuners until she slapped—the second or third time.

KN: I didn't go to that class reunion. I stayed in bed with a good book.

MN: Too bad you couldn't have curled up like a Queen with her handsome Page.

to play her Coming Out Ball at the University Club. By 7th grade she knew life's a thinking sport. Philya's about two inches and twenty pounds smaller than I am but she knows how to block and check. Here, hold these."

She slides her watch and bracelet into his jacket pocket. She unsnaps her purse and hands him a bottle, waving him to the bathroom for paper cups. She crosses one beige leg over the other so her gray skirt covers her knees. "If you forget to give back my valuables I'll show up at your parents' house Christmas Eve with a pillow that makes my sweater puff out. That'll give the Taylor Family something to talk about while you open presents…. Don't you know how to break the seal and pour?"

He figures she wouldn't have invited him here just for a drink. He leans the unopened bottle on the seat and puts a hand on each of her yellow shoulders, finding the oxford cloth starchy like butcher's paper.

She pushes him away. "Down boy! What makes you think we can play that game now? Or do you think you're the team trainer? Drink up."

Joe looks at her as though he's a freshman lineman run over by a senior fullback.

"The problems of friends depress me, until I can figure out what to do about them," Cynthia says.

Joe shrinks back into the seat. "Did she say anything about me?"

"Some. We talk."

Thicker snow spreads through woodlands making the compartment snug, but smoky. She pours, without dripping on her skirt. "Think fruit trees and you'll groove with this. We've got plenty and I'm done studying." She kicks off her heels, pulling at the darker crescents around her toes and straightening the seams that run up the back of her legs.

She balances her cup on the seat to take off her yellow shirt. The charcoal cashmere under it fits like a leotard, a dark icing without wrinkles that spreads over more fullness than he has faced. She *must* know her straps show.

"I see you like my ensemble. Write this down. Sweater: Lord and Taylor—triple-ply cashmere with brass buttons. Skirt: Saks—tweed with pleating and pewter buckle. Would make a good Christmas gift for someone you care about. Know anyone like that?"

She pours again. "Do you know you're a whistler?" she asks. "Not music, mostly hissing."

"*Whistler?*"

"You make a noise like you're working on your car. You hissle!" She swings her legs down the seat. "Makes me feel you're not concentrating on *moi*. You're nice, I'm nice. Let's remember that."

She adjusts her seams again.

He realizes her compartment has a lot more space than the back seat of Amy's mother's car. "You play about every sport, I guess. Amy wrote me that."

"Let's say I can run up and down a field and carry or swing a stick. But I'm at home on water. So's my sister Philya. Tops among sailors under 16, and she's only 14. You keeping my jewelry safe?"

He pats his coat pocket.

"Good boy. Notice how scrupulous I'm being for a girl with a reputation and a healthy libido. I don't want to do anything to get between you and Amy."

"I thought maybe you were pissed at something."

"Well if you and Amy don't work out, about the time you graduate Philya will be starting college—maybe Wellesley. They have their own lake for crew."

"How much will your sister cost when she's 18?"

"Plenty! Philya can throw anything, run or sail faster than any other fourteen-year-old. Girl *or* boy. And if she wanted to pull down a 'B' or 'A' average, she could."

"Red hair?"

"Of course. Anything else finishes second."

Cynthia leans across and kisses him, her tongue shorter than Amy's, her teeth spacing different. She pulls out a tissue. "Lipstick's pretty silly."

"Like neckties."

"They're cute. You're cute. I hope you and Johnson can work things out. If not, invite me down to Old Nassau for a weekend. You've bitched up *her* fall semester. Now unless you're desperate, old sporty, I've got to use the john again. Time to return my valuables: the Buckley watch and bracelet set. If you're not here when I come out, I'll assume the train landed or you gave up and went looking for a *public* men's room. See ya, Tiger." She closes herself in the cubicle.

He waits, figuring they have a couple more hours on the train. But when he hears the tinkling of her charm bracelet again he lets himself out before she has time to flush.

Winter '54

Ed says, "No wonder they call this 'The Belt.'"

Joe drives. "The what?" They have stopped once to change a tire along the strip of gaudy steak houses around Hartford, and twice to reposition the sound equipment they're carrying north for the Triangle Club.

"The 'Hair Belt!' No place on earth like a girls' campus. They hide so much of it there."

Saturday morning classes are ending as they park in Northampton on Green Street between what Ed identifies as Lawrence and Tyler Houses. Girls pedal from classes in Hatfield to the stacks in Smith's Neilson Library, weighted by books and silver and gold forged into rings and rippling necklaces.

Joe's amazed by the sleek luster, the sudsed and brushed bobs and curls. The pageboys, ponytails, permanents, naturally-straight or carefully-conditioned black and blonde locks. The auburns. And every imaginable shade of brown.

The sun tops the hill by the gardens and greenhouses above the pond and boathouses. Eyes sparkle and noses shine through powder and dabs of cream. Bright casually posed princesses murmur confidentially about unending opportunities.

Most possess decisive smiles, firmly set lips, and a capacity to chirp monosyllables in several registers. The sparkle looks as though it really leads somewhere. Someone calls out, "To Rahar's." Others pick up the cry and a group breaks off to cross to the iron Grecourt Gates, where the campus heights drop to the town where Coolidge once sat on his front porch.

A girl still in makeup from the Rally Day show yells to some Deltas from Amherst to make a refreshment run. Ed says, "That's pronounced Am-erst." The girl pulls off her sweater, peeling down to her blouse to face the winter sun and Paradise Pond with its donut hole island. The slope drops so steeply that on a sled the girl couldn't stop before hitting water or cracking up on rocks. Paradise Pond is not wide or deep and reminds Joe of the 10th hole at Minneapolis Golf Club where he caddied for the National Amateur. Forty strong strokes would take a swimmer from the shore to the wooded island; another forty to the far shore below the pre-Civil War State Hospital, enormous with its wings on a hill higher than the college's.

Couples party on the banks and girls without dates meet guys who tracked over from Amherst or drove north from New Haven. Joking that it's the easiest way to meet the required year of Phys. Ed., two girls teach their dates duck-pin bowling, trying to keep the balls from rolling into the water. Laughter overwhelms a girl who announces, "Nasser seized Egypt and the Communists took Dien Bien Phu."

A rangy girl blows a bugle and a slurred voice announces Rally Day awards for "Partied Longest," "Bought Fewest Books," "Used Dorm Room Least." Down the slope a close-harmony group sings:

> How's your father?
> How's your mother?
> How's your Sis-ter Sue?
>
> And while I'm asking,
> How's your family?
> How's your...old...wa...zoo?

A senior wearing a dental retainer, warmed in tweed and cashmere, giggles to her boyfriend, "Nothing's impossible." A Williams' boy tackles her so the three become a slippery, rolling, sun-tanned sculpture.

Joe suggests that he and Ed set up their sound equipment in Scott Gym for the upper class Triangle Club members who will perform at the dance. "Let's do it," Ed says, "but pass me a pitching wedge. I want to drop one on that island and see if I can get down in two putts."

They walk the heights above where water leaves the pond to drop over the dam and continue as a stream. Joe watches two girls in lemon and silver tunics and knickers, the freshman colors, lacrosse sticks high, sleeves rolled above their shoulders, climbing the hill to the gym. They exchange and cradle passes until by the gym door they clomp their cleats against the wall and disappear in muddy socks under the door's overhang.

Once they've finished setting up equipment, Joe and Ed join the girls pulling guys down the hill to town. They pass the Academy of Music, with its classic pilasters and baroque scrolls and ad for *From Here to Eternity*.

Abruptly on the bluff top to the right, they stop and face Rahar's, a tradition sung about all over the East. They say freshmen get served here all the time.

Joe pictures the bluff breaking off, as he looks through a dirty window to see how packed the place is. "*The New Yorker*, right? That crazy Charles Addams?"

"Who he?" a girl asks.

"You don't need to know, but watch out: the folks on the roof are about to pour hot oil on us."

Running a gauntlet of glasses and smoke they bump elbows and step on white bucks to reach a basement table with empty chairs. A hand reaches out. "Well, old sporty, I thought you'd show eventually." Cynthia Buckley offers her firm handshake. "Welcome to Glorious Girl Land." She points to Ed, "Is he any good?"

"Eddie, this is Cynthia Buckley. Cynthia, Ed Walsington. There, did I do that right?"

"I'm Bethesda," Ed says. "You Northrop or Summit?"

"The latter. You a good Quaker boy from Sidwell Friends?"

"Nope!"

"Episcopal?"

"Yup!"

"St. Albans, the National Cathedral where Princeton planted Woodrow in the basement?"

"Oh, he's down there all right, but I live with my dad in Winnetka. I'm New Trier."

"Aha! A Public. Quick, sit down and let's see whether we can get little Joe here to tell us all about Washburn High."

"How did you know I'd be here?" Joe asks.

"How did you know *I* would?" She leans over Ed to shout to a waitress.

A guy wearing a white sweater with a green "D" announces, "I'd never let them take mine!"

A girl with braces says, "We have to."

A girl with braids says, "They won't graduate us without them."

"A guy with a blue "Y" proclaims, "The *Constitution* does not allow that."

"So where do they keep them?" the "D" asks.

"It's unfair. You're defenseless," the "Y" adds.

"Defenseless and very naked. Believe me, it's no treat."

"Can you cover yourself with your hands?"

"If you want to stick around while they take more pictures. Two hands doesn't quite cover it all."

"'Posture Pictures!'" Cynthia explains. The tray of drinks she ordered arrives. "A Smithie tradition. That weenie doesn't know it, but they used to take naked pictures at Yale, Williams, and Amherst too."

The guy at the next table overhears. "I doubt they did that at New Haven."

"They tell us it'll help us stand straight," Cynthia says. "Bullshit! Sports or screwing do more for you."

The girl with the braces says, "They cover you with a sheet and you wait. When they say 'Drop it' you do, and bulbs flash and they snap two profiles, one front, one rear, and you have to come back if anything blurs."[58]

The girl with braids says, "They hold the camera longer when they shoot the front."

The Yalie says, "They should just ask someone who knows you well for a description."

"Like you, sporty? Girls have complained to Adlai and Billy Graham."

Cynthia says, "Big help! Adlai told last year's graduating class that a Smithie's role is to support her husband's career. I wonder whether Adlai stood in the Quad and pictured his audience naked as they prepared to support their husbands. I hear he didn't stick around to take questions."

Ed says, "I told Joe they call this the 'hair belt.'"

Cynthia says, "Well I don't imagine they air brush the posture pictures. My little sister Philya's so perfect that when she was 10 she insisted on showing me a hair. Can you imagine—a *single* hair. Red and straight. I never remember having less than a few. I thought you went from bare to curly overnight. I did and I thought it was because the guy who anchors next to me left something under my pillow for the hair fairy."

Ed says, "It does something to you: sitting here, looking around, picturing."

"Picture this," Cynthia says. "We had a lacrosse scrimmage against the sophs in the rain. Gallons of rain! Field all mud. Us all sponges. But we were ahead 3-2 when they stepped in and stopped the game. Some parent noticed we

---

[58.] MN: Not fair! Wins it two years in a row and Jen Cummings never got photographed without her swimsuit at Washburn's Posture Contest. Never got to show two profiles plus a front and rear.

KN: See, you should have gone to college. And showed up for class at high school now and then.

were running around in soaked white silk, a gauze curtain over a dark background that anyone on the sidelines could see. Black background or red, same difference!"

"So did they give you the win?" Joe asks.

"I think the wet fans won that one," Ed says.

The tables near them clap as the saints come marching in. More bottles get passed. A guy shakes the table he tries to climb on before friends help him up the stairs. Smoke stings Joe's eyes even before Cynthia lights up. Her watchband is now gold, and she's not wearing a Timex.

"That's her," Cynthia points. "Bet she won't stay long. Used to study all the time. Wonder who the guy is?"

Joe looks at the couple. "Too old for a freshman, right?"

"That's Sylvia. She lives in Lawrence House. Terrific brain. She tried to commit suicide last fall by taking pills and crawling under her front porch in Wellesley. She just came back this weekend. She won't graduate with her class, but she'll graduate with highest honors."

The band blasts, swamping the basement with more students who chatter and swallow. Feet tap, fists beat tables. Joe reaches for his wallet. "I gotta go. Can I leave this for the beer?"

"On me!" Cynthia says. "You know, Joe dear, I think it *is* possible for you to avoid becoming a Princeton Charlie."

"Like Joe Cable in *South Pacific*? When he only wants the Seabee Luther Billis to know that he went to college 'in New Jersey.'"

"Like that. You're a quick study when we let you take an untimed test. So why do you waste time stringing wires and all that Triangle Club crap? I'll never make captain of a team because I'm not exactly tactful. But unless I'm winning I want to scream. At the rest of the team. At the wind. At any slob who'll sit on the deck and crew. You're not that slob. You're pretty nice for a male animal. I can see you at UVA— University of Virginia. You'd snow all your roommates' dates. Very southern, a bit too gentlemanly but solidly

Jeffersonian—with hints of self-enlightened, intense, rebel democracy. No, I'm wrong. You care too much. Don't give that up."

"Give what up?"

"Whatever matters to you. Because it's gonna matter to someone else too."

Cynthia shakes her bracelets and asks, "Do you want me to find her? She really needs to see you." Cynthia doesn't wait for an answer but drops some bills on the table and pushes through the crowd.

When he catches up, Cynthia's perched on a stone fountain that surrounds a nude statue with very pointed bronze breasts. "Meet our campus beauty."

Amy stands back in the rain by the plant house. Joe wonders whether he saw her toss away a cigarette and pop in a mint. She comes toward him wearing the vanilla coat with the pockets that have warmed them both at hockey games.

She looks up at him sadly. "It's been so long. I didn't think I'd ever see you. I got a letter from Kathy. Did you?"

"Not recently."

"She says the U sucks."

"How is it here?"

"Awful! For me, anyway."

Cynthia has disappeared.

He holds out his hand, afraid she won't take it. She does, and they walk along the bank above the pond, past the president's house to the street across from the entrance to the QUAD—with all its steps and terraces, Jordan House forming its northeast corner to their right.

At the curb they stop. "Do stockings keep girls warm?"

"They're not so great soaked, but I'd fight for mine when the wind blows up your skirt. They cover you. I wear cotton or wool for classes."

"So?" Joe asks?

"So! Here's where we have to decide. At least one thing. Are we going to spend the night together? Finally?"

Her room in Jordan's shaped like her room at home so familiar objects occupy familiar places. One door opens to a closet by her dresser, its contents clear in his memory; the other to the hallway, an unknown passage.

"Do you like it here?" he whispers, uncertain who can hear and what they might do.

"Sure. As long as our House Mother doesn't burst in."

"Say 'sure' again."

"Surely you heard me."

"You make 'su-re' rhyme with 'pu-re'—two syllables You always have. And that's you. And this is like camp."

"A Kissing Camp," she says, and they do, sitting next to each other on the edge of her bed.

He rubs his hand up and down her calves. "I feel wet silkiness, and they're probably darker now than they will be when they dry. Do you want to take them off?"

"One started off darker than the other. I grabbed them in a hurry. Probably came out with nonmatchers with runners."

"I bet you have everything lined up in your drawers," he says, "Except this." He picks a slip off the rug near her bed.

"I can't believe you're really here. I almost cried myself out, then figured we were finished and everything got hardened: the universe, my pillow, my toothbrush."

"I'm really here."

"How could you have sent that dreadful 'Dear Amy-Joe College' letter? All about 'other worlds' and 'new things that we should explore.' Wasn't I enough? I'm only five hours away."

"It's a hard drive."

"Excuses! Why didn't you answer my letters or call? We could have been like this. Oh, Joe, hold me big."

"You're sure someone isn't going to open that door?"

"What if they do?"

He reaches inside the vanilla coat and presses the front of her dress, hands roaming. "I wonder what these are?"

"They're me, silly." She looks up. "Do you think I'm growing a little—even if it's still more on one side?"

"That's okay. And it's a pretty dress. You're pretty in it. Every time we get together, it's like this, isn't it? Touching you feels unfair—like petting a round bouncy kitten."

"I'll have daddy send a gratuity to Maidenform—and Hanes. My support team."

They drop across the narrow bed so their faces and bodies press. His fingers move inside her dress where her skin feels damp. His hand slides underneath another layer where he traces circles as she lies back on her pillow.

"I'm sorry if I hurt you," he says. "You'll forgive?"

"Sure," she says. "But only once."

"'Su-re' and 'pure'! Do you remember your lavender handkerchief full of Tabu from that small bottle? You smell the same, better than anything. And you're not pouting by the school radiator."

"I have a radiator over there under the window, but I never pout."

She shoots her arms to the ceiling. "Okay, pull!"

He does, and she drops her dress and slip. "Now you have the honor of unhooking my 'Little Angel.' Don't look so serious. That's what they called a training bra, remember?" She presses into his shirt.

He smoothes the silk over her knees, moving higher but stopping where her stockings stop—before the familiar softness, before the familiar curling outside the elastic.

"You always said a girl wore a girdle underneath."

"They wear it on top to show off in clothing ads. Besides how was I to know I was going to run into you? Gracious, such a severe critic! Does it matter as long as I can slide them off—in an emergency? Like this!" She pushes down all her underwear and lets it fall to the rug.

"Now at least you won't catch cold from wet stockings. What color do you call them?"

"'I put them on hours ago for Saturday class. Let's guess at least one of them is 'Clearly Co-Ed.'"

She folds back the sheet and sits. "You've still got on a clothing or two, Mister. Do yourself real fast cause I want to get under the covers."

He takes off his shirt and tie, shoes and socks, trousers. His T-shirt is damp but he takes a quick wipe at his body with it before pulling down his shorts and lying next to her.

They wrap arms and pull into each other. Their fingers and tongues play. But when he starts to roll on top she pushes him back. "Before you hover any closer, I better mention that we might face a problem."

"What's wrong?"

"Nothing we haven't been through. Amy doesn't need to worry much tonight about getting, dare we say the word, 'pregnant,' but...."

"Tonight?"

"...but your former friend's not quite finished with her period. You remember: what we used to call 'that very special part of being a girl.'"

"Damn!"

"We'll figure out something to deal with this not-so-dainty monthly adventure. Or should I say 'curse'? I wish you guys had to bleed. Was it fair that Kathy, not Mickey, got crippled on the fence? A girl in Jordan who comes from Paris says, 'Equal lays, equal bidets.'"[59]

"Will you tell me something?"

"Depends."

"Something about you being here and all. And all the boys' schools. Can I ask you whether...?"

"No!"

"Sorry. And I'm sorry about...your period. Our period!"

"It'll be gone by Tuesday, but so will you. Look, when I saw you standing by the statue next to Lyman Plant House should I have shouted, 'Hey Joe, I fell off the roof Thursday

---

[59]. KN: Ugh! Did you leave that in?
MN: Righto! That *is* as close as we'll come to hearing the Little Princess acknowledge bodily functions—not counting sex. Did you ever hear her say "piss" or "shit"?

after cold cuts and potato salad'? We can still hold each other and kiss and doze. Maybe we can even call that 'sleeping together.' Relax: Jordan House will provide a variety of outlets."

She turns sideways and hugs him hard, reaching below his waist and rolling her fingers rhythmically around him. His palm spreads over her, going as slowly as he can.

Her hand takes a tighter grip as his fingers touch and part her, one finger dipping inside. Then two.

They come close to their usual stopping point where they press their bodies together and rock to release. He assumes they'll stop but doesn't know whether he can, and isn't sure they have to anyway. Their parents are miles away? And if she probably can't get pregnant? He slows the glide of his fingers as they feel a string. He pulls them out, but her hips arch in pursuit. His thumb searches and finds where he thinks she has stiffened. He keeps rolling his thumb and kissing until her shoulders stir and her neck goes rigid. She convulses and releases in spasms, breath sucked away before a tiny cry is replaced by a great calm.

They rest. When she stirs, she goes to her dresser, returning with a plastic compact. She takes out a rubber oval. He has never seen one, but hears her saying, "This is what Petra Malcolm got fitted for last summer. Oops, forgot the tricky part." She goes back for a tube of cream, mostly full.

"You're moving a little fast for me," Joe says sitting up.

"Where have *you* been? We're not back at Washburn. They say this'll keep me from staining you. And you *can* get pregnant during your period. Or the first time you do it. Or if you do it standing up, remember? You definitely can get pregnant when a guy puts it in and doesn't take it out in time, or leaves that little drop that comes out first."

"I suppose I could have bought one of those rubber things—or something—but I didn't know...."

"Here, hold this." She hands him the tube and spreads cream around the rim of the ring before bending the rubber between her thumb and middle finger. "Don't look, promise."

"I'm sorry, but I have to ask…."

"You don't have to. Don't!"

"I mean all this…. You seem to know a lot for someone's who's never…."

"Just lie back. We've waited a long time."

"I need to know. I really do."

"No!"

After scrambled eggs at the green and red diner by the railroad station, Joe and Amy stand under the overhang of the Scott Gym door where yesterday he watched the yellow lacrosse players. Amy's chin looks as though it was rubbed with a raspberry. She wears darker, heavier stockings with blue sneakers. He wears what he wore into her room seven hours ago. He's feeling those awful moments before you leave. Worse: he's feeling what he *did* discover as well as what they *did not* do.

"Do you have to go back?" she asks.

"Ed's waiting."

"Do you *want* to go back?"

"I have so much to do. Don't you? Sunday nights are awful."

They look over the pond, the burbling of water over the falls, the playing fields and hillside leading to the state hospital.

"I wouldn't mind owning all that," he says.

"The father of an Amherst Delt practically does."

"I wish you wouldn't hitch to Amherst or go to all those mixers. I can't believe you're not meeting lots of guys."

"*You* can say that after writing we should 'explore.' Not too consistent, Mister. But I bet when we went to that Calhoun Beach Club Formal you never pictured standing above Paradise Pond with me wearing a Smithie sweatshirt over my diaphragm."

"It's in you? Now?"

"You're not supposed to take it out until…. Figure about dinnertime. About when you'll be pulling into Princeton. Actually I suppose I could take it out now, because you didn't quite put it in. But I'm not about to put on a show out here."

"Can you feel it?"

"I could have felt you in there if you'd let me. We've made lots of good love, even if we haven't 'gone all the way'—yet."

Her perfume and yellow strands envelop him and spread across the hilltop. She's Laurey on an Oklahoma morning. She's Julie Jordan on the Maine Coast as he scratches his nose along her vanilla collar and over her hair until their faces fit and their mouths open.

They feel dizzy amidst dulcet mist.[60] When he lets go, she tosses her skirt high like a curtain so she can reach under to pull down her blouse.

He holds her like a doll, and she can feel him against her. Yet while he holds her he's already charting which subjects he'll study and when he'll fit in extra slave labor time in McCarter Theatre's basement so the tech director will know how hard he's working for a chance at more than pulling nails from flats or scrubbing peeling paint from old drops. And he's confused about last night.

"You're leaving, aren't you?"

"I don't want to, but I need to know, 'Has there been someone…before last night?'"

"Why do you have to ask that? Wasn't last night a dream?"

"Of course it was. But have you ever? If you say 'no'… I'll cheer and die of relief."

"Let's just say. Let's say, that after you didn't write and didn't visit, and didn't…. Anything! Well I found that the farther I went, the harder it was to stop. We found that out together in high school. When I get to a certain point I can't stop—or don't want to." Her words seem to be coming from somewhere across the pond.

"Once? More than once?"

Her voice becomes faint. "Let's say you drop a glass and it splinters. After that…. After that does it really matter how many times you drop it?"

[60.] MN: Enough, already! Those two could shake salt on their cereal and still produce enough body sugar to make it oh, so sweet. I'm surprised he didn't undress her for breakfast. They went back and forth, blowing hot and cold, as she said, but by God this time she was begging for it.

Rain runs down his nose.

"Joe, I'm not a tramp. I'm so sorry."

He wants to be gone and he wants to hug her tighter than anyone has ever hugged. He wants to stay under the overhang of Scott Gym, on the hill above the waterfall, above the donut island on Paradise Pond—for the moment. Because he doesn't know when he will or won't see her again.

Four Years Later—Summer '57[61]

Waves slap Kathy and Joe against rocks in the darkness below Carrie's cottage. Across the bay the ferris wheel sparkles. Off the point friends splash and tease; others picnic in a clearing back in the woods. A rock slips under Kathy's foot but Joe catches her. "Thanks. Even when you wrote you'd never make it through college I had to admit you two made a good-looking couple—whatever wiser voices you finally heeded."

"I listened to you," Joe says. "Always have. Remember when we stood here in 10th grade and watched the girls swim?"

"*You* watched. And it was *one* girl. I heard she'll be here."

"Did you know the original wheel at the Chicago World's Fair carried 1,400 people in one twirl?"

"Is that what you learn in a Princeton math precept?"

Mickey pulls himself from the lake, "Don't touch my sister, fella. I wired her suit. Touch it, and—zap! You're amped. Where's the beer? Where's my blue suedes? Anybody step on them and you'll see a duel." Mickey heads inland toward the fires and iced buckets.

[61.] KN: I'm puzzled that the scenes from here on don't actually appear *within* the Journal itself. They're typed on separate pages. And they sound as though Joe were looking back.

A swimmer they don't recognize pulls herself onto the rocks, slender in the shadow as she unhooks her top and swings it like a stripper before tiptoeing into the bushes, calling out, "Who took my copy of *The Lonely Crowd*?"

Beer cans top the rocks like U-boat targets. A breeze flutters over Kathy's arms as higher waves foam their feet. Joe slaps the water with his palm and wonders where ripples go. Where high school and college went. "Will she be wearing a ring?"

"I haven't seen her. Only talked on the phone with her mother."

"She probably would have made me miserable anyway."

"No comment. Mickey's wrong when he says you're tough. You don't have to be Catholic to be a good worrier. But I don't think she worried until she went through the stages: sadness, anger, real pain. That's what she felt when she had to accept that you were finally leaving her."

"Sometimes I thought...."

"Too much! I'm sorry if I taught you that. You *were* a good-looking couple, and now you can do whatever you want. Me, I'm finally making it to the East."

"I'm glad for you. You deserved to get away four years ago."

"I'm glad for me too."[62]

A hand splashes their rock. A St. Bernard shape pulls up his bulk, shakes, and gropes for a can. "Wet time."

"Down, Luther, down, boy," Kathy says.

"Make it beauty time, my darling duo. Some of these clowns wanna swim across to ride the coaster. I told them, 'There's *no* brew in that park! It's for kids and that wooden coaster collapses every decade. Remember our 6th grade picnic when the girl from over by Roosevelt fell? Remember her screams, then everyone's? Her picture in the *Star*? I'll never

---

[62] MN: You're still puzzled?
KN: Well, this is the first part not in Joe's Journal, but on those typed pages from JO.
MN: JO and Joe? What if Joe knew this JO? What if they talked recently?

forget her face or name: Margo Emmy."

"That happened before the television Emmys," Kathy says. " Sorry, guys. That's sick, isn't it?"

"She stood up," Joe says.

"Yeah, and broke her neck," Luther says. "Kath, can you still get polio from swimming in cold water. Like F. D. R?"[63]

"You're the med student!"

"Not till September."

"Leggy said they had to close Camp Lake Hubert early her last year, but with heroes like Salk and Sabin I think we've pretty well lived through it."

"What a guy, Franklin!" Luther says. "Sitting in his living room corner at Hyde Park, licking those stamp hinges and patting his dog. He let Falla lick some, unless his Scottie was on duty pushing the wheel chair." Luther wraps his big body around Kathy, patting Joe on the back, soaking them both and breathing beer. He places a lineman's hand over Kathy's belly. "No kick here, yet, young lady. I wouldn't worry."

"A little bombed, are we?" Joe says. "I thought doctors had to have perpetually steady hands."

"Steady?" Luther says. "Isn't that what we're supposed to suggest to a nice girl who otherwise wouldn't put out? The night won't always be so young and you two so beautiful. I always thought you made a grand pair. What happened? One of you sterile? Grand night for singing, huh? Hel-lo young lovers."

"*The King and I* tells a strange love story," Kathy says.

"It's *not* a love story," Joe says.

"Oh, but it *is*."

Joe wonders if Amy remembers as he does how this

[63.] KN: Luther would've made a good mate. Bright enough to keep you hopping through every scrap of newsprint, always kind and caring. And best of all he said he loved me. But…the spark wasn't there. I couldn't picture myself under the sheets with him.

MN: "Spark," me love? Does't thou means a-screwing a-times? And if not twixt lawful sheets couldn't you have simply logged more backseat action?

bright slobbery Luther guy kissed her hard and long at graduation between the end of the dance and the dawn breakfast at the Chalet.

Kathy pulls herself up. "Okay, I'll walk to the fire."

"Touchdown! Six points," Joe announces.

"Why not seven?" Kathy asks.

"Can't kick extra points playing knee football."

Kathy asks Luther, "At Yale what did you think about Secret Societies or Harvard's Final Clubs? I never wanted Woody to join, but when he was elected president of the *Crimson* he felt he had to—and probably wanted to by then. He'd rather have been voted president of the *Lampoon*, the humor magazine, but some hotshot named Updike from eastern Pennsylvania got that."

"If you want to know," Luther says, "The club men first try to make sure you're *not* Jewish—at least not too many of you. Second, they find out—which they already know—if you're truly wealthy, or at least from an established family or prep school. Third, they ask their varsity members how well you play football or squash. Finally, I guess they even consider whether you're a decent human being. I passed out cards saying, 'Only the last, thank you very much.'"

The three squeeze between shrubs into a clearing with picnic tables and a blazing fire. Luther gets louder as he rounds up a team to head into Excelsior for more beer. "I'm staying by the fire," Kathy says. "Show me the burger meat and I'll cook up some."[64]

Joe waits as though something more might happen. He sits at a table with Leggy Williams and an older guy he's seen her with. Leggy wants to bring the guy by Joe's lake cabin on the way home to hear Robert Preston and Barbara Cook sing *The Music Man*. During his shower, Joe joined in when Preston threatens to drop marbles on Marian's library floor, but stopped and could only listen when Preston admits there

---

[64.] KN: Do you believe Joe has seen the typed sheets?
MN: I even believe it possible that you're sleeping with Beaver Pond.

are bells on the hill and Cook agrees that seventy-six trombones *did* lead the big parade. Joe feels a capacious sense of something about to happen. He had that feeling years ago in a girl's basement rec room when the gang learned to dance in stocking feet. Those were nights when you might meet someone new and glorious: Pinza's "Stranger across a crowded room," Richard Kiley's "Stranger in Paradise." But he also hears Preston's warning of being left with a lot of empty yesterdays.

"I'll drink to us," Leggy says. "Decent kids, right?"

Joe's back itches and his toes fry from the fire at the same time his head cools from a lake breeze. Fire and ice. Like trying to sleep by a volcano.

Brakes squeal. Figures lug cases from the parking lot by the treeline. And suddenly he sees her.

As she gets closer, he sees that her hair is still pulled back in a ponytail, making her look even younger. She's joined at the waist to a big guy who weaves a bit: Joe's old rival Jim Raleigh, fine golfer and hockey wing at Southwest High and Dartmouth. She's *not* with her Amherst dental fiancée named Farrindon.

Joe's angry and relieved when they move to another group instead of continuing toward him.

Mickey pretends to stagger, but can't quite draw a laugh because he's too realistic. "You bent yet?" he grunts. "That's...question."

Plates piled with food pass around. Cans continue to pop. "I guess I can count a few," Joe says.

Mickey looks at Joe and Luther, disgusted. "You college boys!"

"I got it," Joe says, "You're doing the captain in *Mr. Roberts*?"

"Matter of fact, the doctor. And the doctor prescribes...more of the same." He whips away Joe's mostly full can.

"Shit-faced!" a voice yells from deep in the trees.

"For a truly shit face," Mickey says, "I prescribe plastic surgery. Might as well beef up the boobs too while we've got her on
the table. Get the young lady's clothes off, STAT. That's the way
medical men talk, right Luther? Careful of splinters on that picnic table. I'll slice if someone can figure out how to close."

"What happened to Kathy?" Luther asks.

Mickey asks, "What'd you do to scare her? Dangle your
wanger? No, that wouldn't scare Kathy. She's seen bigger.
Even in our bathroom."

"She did look a little down," Luther says.

"Down? You sly fox. Down on the grass with my vixen
sister?"

"Dumps. She was down. I was down in the old dumper-
oo too. Mick fella, you really *are* shit-faced."

"See that little honey hanging her buns over the coals?
She sings all that Mary Martin crap. Go ask. She'll explain
that '*moi*' rhymes with '*twa*,' obviously short for an anatomi-
cal feature you'll need to know if you're going to open a
practice—or a blind date."

Mickey goes for a fresh can. Joe looks for Kathy. A lime
Frisbee glances off a burning log, spreading melting plastic
through the air. "Ugh!" someone groans. "Kill it." Joe stamps
on it remembering the old prank of putting dog shit in a
paper bag and leaving it burning on a neighbor's doorstep.
Someone pours beer on the Frisbee, and Joe's foot.[65]

Mickey calls out, "Where's my sister? Who's got her? Hot
damn, if she didn't keep a fire under Mr. G. by never letting
him know when we might strike back."

Leggy says, "Yeah, and she still has the scars to show she
did the right thing."

Mickey darts away, bumps a tree, and stops, stunned. "By
the way I heard Mr. G. died, so we won! We got together with
death and pulled out a win. Hot damn!"

Joe looks up when Amy sits on the edge of his table slow-

---

[65] KN: I finally had to walk away: from the fire's heat, Luther's hot flesh
and pants. Mostly from the way Joe stopped talking to me the
moment *she* arrived.

ly sipping. She swings her legs, not paying much attention to Jim Raleigh, or anyone. She's the only girl wearing a dress: a sack, which brushes past her hips and tapers above and below her knees

"Nice place," Amy says sounding as though she doesn't care whether she's heard.

"It's a zoo! Sorry, I don't mean *that zoo*."

"How about Humplemeyer's across the road? We sat there awhile. All that German food: gross!"

"How have you been, really?"

"Me? Oh, you could say cute, cozy. What's the right answer?" She continues to look past him.

"How're your folks? Your dad's quite a guy."

"Yes he is. So how you doing?"

Before Joe has to answer Mickey slops his hands all over Amy's bare shoulders and drips on her dress. "Magnificent! You two are *magnifico*. *Magna cumo*. Two great kids, two great educations. Doing a wonderful job. Back home with us, Amy? What can I do for you? Mick-off, perhaps? Done! But like General Mac said, 'I shall return!'"

"You don't have to go," Amy says.

"I want to tell ya how good ya look."

"Thanks," Amy says staring into the woods.

"If I tell ya I like your figure, will ya hold it against me?"

"Come on!" Joe interrupts.

"…or give me a bust in the mouth?"

She says softly, "No, thank you."

"Take off!" Joe says, noticing for the first time that Frankie Hill sits alone in the shadows wrapped in a blanket.

"I'll write everyone letters of 'pology in the morning." Mickey bows and wanders off, turning back to ask, "Can someone point me to the bushes? I think the bard's producing outdoor theater: *Toilet and Crashdadoor*."

Amy sits primly, holding a can above the dress covering her knees. When she brings the can to her mouth Joe thinks it covers too much of her. She has tied her straw ponytail in a blue ribbon high on her neck. Something else strikes him.

As Kathy said she is *not* wearing a ring. *Any* ring. And she has no tanning line on the finger of her left hand.

"You look great," he says.

"So do you. Still playing 35 holes a day?"

"When I can. Work some. Wait!" He shifts closer to her, raising his arms.

Startled, her eyes widen. "What's wrong?"

"Nothing, but it's not there. I missed it at first and didn't realize it."

"Did I forget to button my dress?"

"You forgot your spot. Your beauty mark. You don't have it. It should be here!" He starts to touch her.

She doesn't draw away but turns her face so only the left side shows.

Around the fire a voice sings about a "Silvery Moon." Others ask, "How High?" modulating into "Moonlight Bay," "Harvest Moon" and "In the Evening." Above the fire, above the ferris wheel, over all of the bay, so many stars hold their place around a single moon.

Kathy has returned to lean against Luther. Most have stopped paying attention to Mickey spraying beer cans.

Amy sits on the table edge watching the flames and swinging her legs, swinging and sipping, not quite in time to the music.

Mickey flops against a tree and watches Frankie. And watches Joe watch Amy.

"So? So she's getting married and moving to Philadelphia?" Mickey scuffs a practice ball inside the fence at Hiawatha. "Trap her here or fly there before the young lovers do too much consuming—or do I mean consumating? I'll ask Connie Mack to save you seats at Shibe Park if you want to talk this over with him and Dick Sisler. Dick's really got an 'in' since his ninth inning homer brought Connie the pennant. I'd invite Rich Ashburn to sit in too—he's a comer. Three should cover the bases. If you get on the stick you can have it made in the shade. But if you wait for the lovers to hit Philly you're gambling that her dentist's lousy in the sack—however fine his fingers might be in the mouth."

"I don't know what to do," Joe says.

"Tell her she's making a shit-ass mistake. *If* you really think she is. Tackle the fucker! Take tongs to his teeth! But stop talking, will you? You made me fade that shot into the trees."

Joe strokes another ball that lands on the fairway between the fence and a stream that angles toward the distant thirteenth green. He ignores cars passing on the Parkway, concentrating only on smoothness and tempo. The tee where they dump their practice balls year-round rises like a mountain above the sunken twelfth green. Joe counts, "One-and-two," connecting so squarely he knows the ball will soar, drop, and bounce over the dried turf.

"Why am I not hitting for shit?" Mickey asks.

"Try not sliding your left hand so far under." Joe drops his nine-iron on his bag and pulls out an eight, raking more balls toward him, wondering whether this late in the day a group will want to play through and interrupt their practice. "Do you think I made a mistake?"

"We haven't found out whether your coaching about my left hand's worth anything and you've changed the subject back to her. With the wedding less than a month off, why not ask her out? Get gutsy, guy! Sure, you might come away with a double bogey—or worse. But hell, pull out a lot of club and go for it."

"How can I ask her out now?"

"Try the telephone or wrap a leg around her pins and cut her down on the front lawn. It's not creeping bent but it's far enough from the second floor that her daddy will never make those steps in time to stop you. Maybe he doesn't want to. Hump her until she sings *Carmen* or calls, 'Uncle, break off my fuckin' engagement.' Or do you like picturing her getting drilled by a weenie dentist?"

"Stop, okay!"

"Hurts, right? Let's go to your place and pop a beer. Maybe you'll get it off with a climactic sneeze." Mickey addresses a ball with his driver. "Tee 'er high and let 'er fly. Play a Pogo and pull out a seven when you used to need a five-iron." He takes the club away with a jerk, coming in way under, sending the ball skyward so it floats a few seconds before dropping ninety yards away in the creek. He bangs the head of his driver, then plucks a tuft of grass to wipe off the white stain. "Hell, did you hear we're gonna let Japan back into the National League, or is it the League of Nations? People forgive and go on. You want a girl; you can't have her. You get a girl; and you don't want her—or she doesn't want you. That can go on forever."

Joe glares. "After going out every weekend for two years we sent her that letter from college breaking it off."

"*We*, Romeo? You were the star. Kathy and I only get supporting credits for that letter."[66]

---

66. KN: Okay. Time to tell me all about that letter.
    MN: Not to worry. I simply asked you to fix a few sentences. You never knew who it was going to or who it was from.
    KN: Joe to Amy, right? You bastard!
    MN: He asked for it. Sorta.
    KN: And you never told me?
    MN: Did you ever ask? Look, I figured I was clearing the field: giving you a better chance.
    KN: Oh, thanks a whole lot of a heap. That's the Journal chapter you hid from me, right? You're a rotten piece of shit! And as your twin, I wonder what that makes me?

Joe flips a ball left-handed with his sand wedge and catches it in his practice bag. He pronates the wedge outward to keep building his left wrist and arm muscles. He peels off his glove. "Whenever we were together we touched more than we talked. We assumed! Maybe we should have planned."

"I watched you in 7th grade try to reach across three rows to touch those titty buds. Did you two ever get fornisatisfaction?"

Joe snaps his glove in Mickey's face.

"A duel! Hot damn! We are going to have a fucking old-time duel. You name weapons: woods or irons? Or do you want to trade knuckle sandwiches? I bet you're defending what you hope she's still got. And you know, guy, what she's got down there's no different from what any girl's got. They got majors *and* minors and for awhile they have, what Kathy calls, *teenaga intacta*. Whose purity really bothers you: hers or yours?"

Joe slams a fist into Mickey's jaw. Joe winces from the pain in his hand as Mickey drops, almost grinning, blood bubbling from his lip and nose.

Joe sinks to his knees. Mickey wipes his mouth on Joe's glove. "Was that good for you too, Joe?"

"Hell, I'm sorry."

"Should be. Even if I dispatch my insurance people to estimate damages—which I won't, having no insurance—I don't think medical expenses will be a problem. I can go straight to her dentist friend for repairs."

"Lawrence Humphrey Farrindon! She told me, "You oughta come over and meet 'Larry.' I haven't."

"She's not in a grave yet and it's death that provides a touch of the overwhelming. Tell her all the stuff you told me. Tell her the stuff that used to drive Kathy up the Washburn wall. Because of you, my sister used to walk with a perpetually avocado pallor and a small-scale stiffness in her drawers."[67]

---

[67] KN: I find your description offensive, and hardly accurate. Obviously you're not the girl twin. But at least you said "stiff" not "hard."

"What if she rejects me?"

Mickey slams his driver into his bag, rattling clubs like thunderclaps. "That's it, isn't it? You're not willing to take a risk that she might reject you. How horseshit can you be? How many times did you reject her? All your breathy whispers and then, 'See ya 'round.' Sure, she might tell you to screw off. Maybe she should. But until the minister speaks you can still decide whether you'll stick. Joe my man, you need to risk your unblemished season. And by the way, this is your day to buy the beers!"

"Why me?"

"Because you've depressed the piss out of me. Hell, I'll toss in a buck if you don't screw away all afternoon looking for every lost ball. And when you see Kathy don't bring up that letter. She'd feel like a shit if she ever found out that she helped."[68]

---

[68] KN: Well: end of secret! And, indeed, I certainly do feel like a shit.

"Why?" Kathy asks Joe. "It doesn't make sense! Why now? You never tried to touch me in high school. Was it that half-gallon of dreadful red we lugged up here?"[69]

"Did you scream? Somebody screamed last night." Joe lies under Radisson Hotel sheets not sure whether head or stomach will fail first. The room lurches; the whirlies lurk. He *does* feel spent, but not at all heroically.

He can't see much from under a pillow but notices a contestant's ribbon of light reflecting across Kathy's abdomen above the jagged marks that cross from hip to ankle.

"Your call to meet in the Viking Room before I flew east surprised me. I thought you wanted us to listen to Hildegarde sing. I hardly expected you to hand me a room key."

She sits up, not bothering to cover herself as she twists toward him in a tangle of sheet. She scratches her orangish snarl with unpainted nails while he tries to keep her in focus. He starts to count her clothes on the floor, her rosary beads on the bed table, giving up when she asks, "You all right?"

"Wine's worse than beer. While we drank that rotgut did you watch the label dissolve?"

"You wanna get sick? You might feel better."

"No! Well, maybe."

"Barf it all up. You won't feel wonderful, but what did you expect? You are *not* having a heart attack. If you were I'd have stuck tubes in your veins, pumped blood in or sucked it out, depending on how nice you were acting."[70]

---

[69] KN: Hold on! I told you to trash this scene. This is *not* an episode that matters to the story of Joe or our friends. I can't imagine JO could have come up with it. Unless he did talk to Joe. Be decent, brother. I might not feel so strongly if there were other times. But I had only this once.

[70] MN: Did "Wonder Boy" ever *not* act nice to you?

KN: No, but he never acted the way I wanted him too—except that night. So it's probably more true that you left this scene in—naked as it makes me feel.

MN: It shows that you two finally fucked.

KN: Stop!

MN: More than once, true?

KN: Well, until he passed out. And later. And in the morning.

"Remember that coach out west who keeled over in a hotel room with a honey?"

"I'm not a honey and it's not your heart. You wait and you'll rally."

"I guess I was a little high."

"I *guess* you were."

"I didn't even notice whether they watched us get on the elevator. I remember the Viking ship swinging over the bar and Hildegarde finishing a set and looking for the Men's Room. Me looking for one I mean. Did I claw you? Climb after you like a beast who hadn't eaten in years?"

"You *do* know how to phrase things to make a girl feel grand."

"I guess it was bound to happen, sooner or later."

"I always assumed later, much later—or never. I saved myself for you—almost."

"I guess I'm flattered."

"I thought last night was kinda nice. When we got under the sheets. Skin on skin, nothing between."

"Air."

"And the cute little foil packet you let me tear open. Yuck! All oiled and slippery. Better to take a chance and have a kid. Or do you still worry about getting a nice girl 'in trouble'?"

"I've worried since 7th grade, when I'm not sure I could have gotten anyone in trouble."

"And you never did, right?"

"Kath, you remain a novelty: the good girl! I think—don't you—when we look back, this will be a…truly good moment."

"Can we call them 'moments'?"

"Did I mention 'love'?"

"Oh yes, you chattered like a squirrel, 'I love you, love you, always loved you, so it's okay, okay.' I helped you put it in the first time but when I looked through your trousers and found that frugal Joe came to the Radisson with only one rubber I got a little nervous. But, oh well, I figured the next few times your count would be going down so the more we did it the less the risk. I even spent the time you were asleep figuring out how to explain to Father Doyle. I plan to stress nudity, which is less than a venial sin, the kind they don't forgive as easily."

"I apologize for dozing off."

"'Dozing'? You 'crashed.' Your route covered bottle to bed to me to bathroom and back. I kept humming, 'Don't fall asleep,' that lovely melody Rosemary O'Reilly sings in *New Faces of 1952*. Remember? She's lying next to a man, passed out because he's had a little bit too much to drink. And she wants to tell him how grateful she is that he's in her bed. That he's her husband and it's their first anniversary. I felt like that. Tell me: if Amy had been in the next room would you have stayed with me?"

He pauses, wiping his mouth on the pillow, wanting to say it right. "I'm sure I heard a scream down the hall. Didn't you?"

"I heard. It was the woman in the Charles Addams number sealing her husband in the wall."

"I think I asked whether we should call somebody. What did we do?"

"You kept peeling off my dress and unfastening my stockings, ruining half a pair of good nylons. One stocking disintegrated like the label on the wine bottle."

"Were you the one who screamed?"

"Me scream? With you here? I can always sing 'Onward, Christian Soldiers,' and a trooper with sunglasses will gallop me to confession. But I loved last night. Loved *you*. I have always loved you, but you've always known that."

"We've been close."

"You made me wobble before I learned to limp. How bad *does* my side look? With clothes, I can almost pretend it never happened." She strokes one hand over his face while the other brings his hand back into her orangeness. "'Best equipment in town,' remember? We always joked that you had 'the best equipment in town'—with no idea what we meant."[71]

"If the Radisson's good enough for the Kingston's Trio, why not me?"

"Would you feel better if I suddenly turned into You-Know-Who? Little Miss Perfect? Sorry! Oh, I love you so. Do you wonder when we're close like this where one person stops and the other starts? Or where passion comes from and where it goes? Don't answer."

He doesn't move as the air conditioner blows across their damp bodies. With the wedding three weeks away he figures Amy must be wearing an engagement ring right now.

"Want to sleep?" she asks. "Some breakfast?"

"Couldn't eat a thing."

"Like the spook in Charles Addams looking at the baby and telling the nurse, 'Don't wrap it, I'll eat it here.'"

"I guess sending the letter was the right thing."

"Oh, bury that letter!" She rolls away, yanking at more sheet.

"Should we worry about babies?"

"No, we should *not* worry about anything. Pretend it's the seventh day when God told you to rest."

"That's kinda what I mean. Should we be counting? Is this a good time for you?"

"It's a *wonderful* time. A wonderful life!"

"I mean a good time for you to...."

"Make babies? Yeah! It happens to be perfect. But the odds are always against it, and you can say 'baby' rather than 'babies.' Good Catholic girls can make lots of those but generally one a night—not counting the five Dionnes up in Canada."

[71.] MN: You knew!

KN: Well, I knew I could pin Joe, punch him around like Joe Lewis until 7th grade. I'd do anything for him. And he'd do anything for me—except the one thing I really wanted.

"So this is a good time for you?"

"Depends on what you want. I'm assuming you do *not* want me to have a baby. Now or in the near future. Let's see —I'm not supposed to know much about this, but counting from ovulation to conception this is as good a time as I could pick. I don't get much more fertile. I should have told you, but I didn't do the math until now. Don't sweat it. Look, last night means a lot to me but I'm not planning to have a baby over it."

"But you could?"

"I could, but anything we say or do won't make any difference. We're old friends, right? Let's not do anything to lose that."

"I could love you," Joe says.

"Wouldn't it be pretty to think so? Who said that? Another Kathy? No, I guess not. Anyway, you probably won't reach that stage, will you? No love story, huh?"

"So what do we call this? What would your mother say? She's always been a fan of mine, but.... This might be too much surprise."

"Or what she's always hoped for."

"Telling my folks sounds grim. And getting in the phone booth with Father Doyle won't be any picnic for you."

"I don't like it when you make fun of the church. The rest of the world's bad enough. Please leave Rome alone."

"Sorry. So what do we call last night?"

"Don't call it anything. Feel good about it."

"I feel fine. How about you?"

"I feel fine now, but awful when Mickey finally told me about that letter. Believe me, I did *not* know. Mickey came to me with a few of his chicken tracks and I found myself filling in real words."

"You shouldn't blame yourself?"

"No? Well listen to the worst part. I *enjoyed* writing it. Mickey didn't say, but I guessed he was helping you write

Amy. I like Amy. We grew up together. But, oh, how I envied her. I'm so, so sorry.[72]

"It did seem pretty articulate coming from Mickey."

"I made a mistake getting between you and Amy. I shouldn't have done that."

Joe watches her cry. He rolls over, and when he wakes, wonders where he is.

She showers, then stands next to him putting on her make-up. She tosses both stockings away. She rubs his shoulder as he dresses. He looks at the rough redness of her eyebrows. He remembers the warm hunger with which she kept her legs either high in the air or around him, and he remembers the cold descents. He wonders how things will go for Kathy when she flies east. He wonders whether Amy will follow as planned in three weeks. After a dozen years living two houses from Kathy, and half-a-dozen years seldom-separated from Amy, he is about to watch each of them leave.

And last night, each time he and Kathy stopped moving together, he found himself back in a strange hotel bed, tangled and very much alone.

---

72. KN: So the letter and the night at the Radisson probably *do* belong in any fair reconstruction of your Journal, Joe.

MN: If that's settled, it's time for you to explain "Country Matters." Not the whole book—that's beyond me—just the title.

KN: It's from *Hamlet*. Write this down: Act III, Scene II, lines 119-123. That's where, in front of all the court—his mother and uncle, the new King and Queen, her fool of a father—Hamlet treats Ophelia rudely. As though she were a country sloven.

MN: Like one of them slut-types?

KN: Not far from the mark. And even you picked up, way back in Footnote 1, that when he asks to lie in her lap he's really playing on the meaning "lay." In fact "Country Matters" refers to…crude, uncivil copulation.

MN: You mean like you and Joe under the Radison sheets?

KN: I'd prefer you not make comparisons. That meant something.

MN: Something civil?

KN: It will always mean much to me.

MN: A good screw usually does.

KN: Would you please take a long walk on….

MN: …a short dork? I mean dock? Minnetonka or White Bear? Buy me a case of Hamm's and you're on. And thanks for the lesson. Now I know all about publishing, Shakespeare, and screwing in the country or a city hotel. I already knew about picking deer ticks off tits.

Through the screen Joe recognizes familiar cracks in the oak door before it swings away from him. He hesitates, "Dr. Johnson?"

"I believe I already gave at the office."

"This is Joe. Joe Taylor. Remember?"

"Not your number. Football?"

"No numbers. Golf! How are you? Is Amy free?"

"Which would you like to know? She's not going to be free much longer, but if she invites you to the big show don't bring presents. Got enough of those. As for me, I operate less often."

"That's good."

"*That's* a little *angina pectoris*."

"I didn't know that."

"Neither did I until I bent over after duck hooking a three-wood."

"You're taking care of yourself?"

"I prefer letting Marie do that. She's asking for overtime and probably will get it. Did you care to speak with the bride or mother of?"

"She's not married yet?"

"Formalities have yet to be observed. I'll be supporting her for another—what fine families from Philadelphia apparently call a—fortnight. Come in. As I recall you were one I liked: never opened my icebox without asking. Maybe you can still save her from listening to that young man talking bitewings over dinner. I never used to talk gall bladders."

"I wanted to…say hello."

"Imagine talking incisors while chewing Thanksgiving turkey. Even barbers cover more territory. By the way, Marie says I'm supposed to congratulate you for some award."

"Just for sportsmanship."

"Just that? I suppose we already have enough of that. Well, I hear footsteps on the stairs. Did I remember to tell you to get her home on time?"

Amy enters as though nothing has changed since the first night she descended twirling her straw ponytail above precarious daffodil pumps.

Riding toward the alumni party at Lake Minnetonka, Amy leans against the door in a sleeveless black shift that leaves her knees uncovered except for misty non-Lutheran stockings. She rests her head against the window, a long way from his lap.

He motions behind. "You can open that now or wait. It's *not* a wedding present."

"For me?" Her voice livens as she brings the package to her lap. Before opening it she takes a silver case from her purse, picks a cigarette, and snaps a silver lighter engraved "AF." Joe tightens his gut. Fuck Larry Farrindon! Fuck smoking!

She kicks off her heels, tucking her stocking feet beneath her shift. A blue and white bathing suit lies between them. She points. "Turn on the gravel and keep going." Resting her cigarette on the ashtray she finally pulls the bow off the package. "Will I be surprised?"

"You might be." He wants to get his head underwater, relax with a few beers, not feel so squirrely.

She looks inside. "I've waited a long time for one of these."

"I thought you might already have one."

"Not in black." She drops the heavy sweater with its orange "P" over her swimsuit. "Turn! That driveway toward the lake."

Amy disappears into the poolhouse leaving Joe to scan miles of lakefront, acres of lawn sloping to shrubs, bushy, sharp-clipped, backing full-flowered cutting borders around a privately Olympian patio and pool.

Joe changes before Amy reappears in her striped suit, bright as the flower borders. She has tied his present, the black sweater with the orange "P," around her waist.

Joe's soul sails as they rudder between tables, then sinks as she accepts a drink and drops into a recliner next to a man who says he went to Princeton with Jimmy Stewart. "Jim played the accordion. Wasn't much of a talker but could sing a little, and married a wonderful girl. *Wonderful Life.* Remember that one?"

Joe drops into chlorine to paddle past a woman in a vegetable suit who presses a Hamm's can to her belly like a periscope. An orange and black mermaid, goggled and finned, strokes past. He retreats from her flutter kicks, scraping his chest when he pulls himself out to hunt for an ice tub and church key.

His host, sporting an orange and black Class of '32 twenty-fifth reunion jacket, imprisons Joe in a storage shed near the poolhouse to interview a goalie with a B average, whom the Alumni Association bused all the way down from the Iron Range. Joe asks the fellow how he feels about school, listens, and suggests that he also consider the University of Minnesota branch at Duluth or Hamline if he wants a city college. By the time Joe escapes, bodies clog the water.

Mr. Alumnus continues his pursuit. "Did I make a proper introduction? My wife and I naturally extend our warmest welcome to 'Never Doon.' Like Brigadoon, only Episcopal, not Irish. Good old John here...."

"It's Joe, Sir."

The chairman's wife interrupts, "Miles loves to open our home to Princetonians at least once a year. You've got Gersch Hall on campus, but we want you to have the Gersch home here. We're planning to bring either the hockey team or the Tigertones out at Christmas. Miles played squash with Mel Ferrer."

"Jose, Peggy. Mel's younger, the one with Audrey Hepburn. Joe's my class."

"Miles has his whole office here every Christmas. Men who drive trucks, ladies who clean, whatever faith each professes." She gestures at terraces near the mansion and groves of hardwood and pine beyond. "You probably guessed that Miles and I are to blame for all of this. We were fortunate to have the means to improve on nature. Please call me 'Margaret.' Later if I ask you to call me 'Peggy,' you'll know I've had too many cocktails or been smitten by youthful charm."

Joe plops into the pool just as the orange and black mermaid backstrokes by. She winks over an armpit and slows to tread water. "I'm Wellesley. But only Class of '62. I'm a sub-freshman now. Be a freshman this fall. I'm Summit—and White Bear."

"I used to know someone from there. Fine athlete."

"My sister, Cynthia! She told me to watch out for you. I'll tell her you're cute but hard to catch. She said you're hard to understand too. Do you have speech impediments? I'm Philya Buckley. Cynthia had all her Summit friends in stitches over the ride you two took in her compartment home from Chicago freshman Christmas."

"She mentioned that? She was generous to share her space."

"Oh, yeah, she mentioned it. And how you partied it up at Rahar's Ralley Day. By the way, I've grown another red one since then."

"Red one?"

"Never mind. I'd ask you to fetch me a drink—maybe later I will—but right now I'm waiting for that dreamy butler with the Belafonte brow. They're keeping the poor guy close to scoop goose poop from the pool."

Amy, suit still dry, smokes with a different old guy wearing a different tiger-patterned blazer. "Only great non-Jew composer? Cole Porter! And he was a Yalie! Also what we used to call 'a little *light*.' You have to give them credit though. Hell of a heritage! Rodgers, Lerner and Lowe, the Gershwins, Irving of course, and now this young longhair Len Bernstein. Back in college Brooks Bowman took the prize. A lyrical Nordic God! A musical Hobey Baker! Damn

guy got himself killed in a car wreck the summer he graduated or you'd have heard from him."

Joe wants to say, "Did you know, asshole, that Porter has
a section in 'My Heart Belongs to Daddy' that's an eleven-bar
Yiddish cadenza?"

Mrs. Gersch gushes, "All our friends think the Twin
Cities are quite special—especially White Bear and
Minnetonka. So much beauty. So few problems. Almost no
coloreds, and all our clean lakes."

Joe feels sweaty from lateness. He hasn't had his chance to
say what he's planned to say to Amy. And on the pool edge,
the black sweater with the orange "P" hangs half in the water.

Suddenly she's next to him, shaking out lemony tufts
pasted to her ears. "Been in the pool much?"

"Plenty! Let's get the hell out of here."[73]

---

73. KN: Do you realize how young we were then?
     MN: Summer of '57? Free, white, and twenty-two!
     KN: Michael! I only spoke of age. Stifle your careless prejudices!
     MN: We were both twenty-two. Joe too. Amy only twenty-one.
     KN: And you realize how old we are now?
     MN: Can't count higher than sixty. Don't want to.
     KN: Even though they say life expectancy might be up to seventy-
         five, even eighty: do you realize that means we've lived more
         than three-quarters of our lives? More than that.
     MN: So?
     KN: So, I don't like to think about that. Ten, maybe fifteen years?
         That's not a whole lot left.
     MN: Same for Joe and Amy. Wherever the hell they are. At least in the
         Journal we can watch them. And Joe's getting closer and closer to
         Amy's front door. Not the dead end he wants.

Heading for the strip of land along Gray's Bay where Minnehaha Creek begins its flow across all of south Minneapolis to the Falls and the Mississippi, Joe looks for the lights of Excelsior, where they used to ride the ferris wheel and push cotton candy in each other's face. He feels his swimsuit soaking his pants as he considers places ahead where he might stop and park. He pictures the dead end, just past her house by Pearl Park.

"Don't get me lost—or late," Amy says. "Daddy might stand up in church and object that Larry's not Lutheran, or a surgeon, or a Washburn graduate."

Joe scouts the shoreline, buoyed as he hums. Will she whistle with him as she used to when Robert Preston and his Librarian finally blend "Seventy-six Trombones" with "Bells on the Hills"?

Miles later, he passes a stretch he recognizes as the golf course at Orono Orchards. Cows chew and stare. He speeds up, a tire squeaks, she glares. Does she realize that he's been mistakenly driving *away* from the city?

After two hours of opportunity tossed away he still has to retrace the miles back past "Never Bloom"—or whatever the hell it was—where they'll still be forty minutes from her house. She twirls a shoe on her toes. He feels the breeze that ripples the down on her arms. As they pass under a light, he finally sees it. Not enormous, but definitely a diamond. Right there on her finger—sparkling at him like a bad joke.

Once on a familiar road east, he barrels over highway. She adds his towel to hers to hide goose bumps. "If you still have your swim suit on," she says, "I bet you're frozen stiff." He looks over at her and she looks away out her window. "I didn't mean it that way."

He counts each click of the odometer, each click of her lighter. They pass the canyon below the first tee at Edina where they belly-flopped in the blizzard at the Y party. He follows 50th Street, past the Edina Theater, Nolan's, the Hasty Tasty. He stays on 50th where an addition to the Creek leaves Lake Harriet to increase the flow to the Falls and the River. They pass Washburn, with its fenced field and long row of poplars.

He brakes at the Nicollet light, now less than a mile from her house. He wonders what she'll do if he pulls into one of their old parking places. Maybe she won't notice if he keeps going straight to Portland and takes a right. He can pass the Thomas Heggen House and drive to the end of Pearl Park, take another right and stay next to the park with Diamond Lake on their left. At Hampshire another right turn will take them—as it has so many times before—the two long blocks to the dead end circle. Once there, he can turn the car back to face the lake. With houses only on their right, they can settle back and look across the open parklands of Pearl, secure that no car can reach them that they won't see.

A car honks at him. The light has turned green. Joe takes his foot off the brake and bumps over the streetcar tracks and up the curve to 1st Avenue, past Jeff Hatch's house and up the street from Leggy's. He drops down the first hill in 50th's triple ski jump, straightens, then drops twice more.

But where the Parkway joins 50th, he forgets to go straight to Portland, automatically turning right at the sandstone bridge with the squat pylons where they used to sit. Annoyed, he races his motor so it roars and echoes over her neighborhood. But going this route he can still get to the dead end where he can reach out, grab her, and say, "We have to talk."

He turns left on 51st and immediately takes a right up the Tarrymore hill. But he automatically circles her block, turning down Luverne rather than taking Clinton to Hampshire. He lets the engine die on the slope above 5106. The big pine still masks the light in her father's den.

Amy hugs her purse and towel. No sweater: Joe last saw that hanging over the edge of the pool. She has her hand on the passenger door.

"Wait!" He wants to shout, "I want you to break that engagement!"[74]

She turns, impassive. "What?" The hand with the ring opens the passenger door.

"Remember?"

"What?"

"Remember...." From so much what should he choose? Daffodil silk and shiny heels reflecting a straw ponytail? A basement lit only by TV after the College Boards? Her Smith dorm room? Alone in the zoo on a night with snow melting and buds so close to opening? A glass dropped more than once so it no longer mattered? Unsure, he chooses: "Your dating blouse!"

"Goodnight, Joe."

"Remember your dating blouse? All stretched around the neck? You'd wear it with nothing underneath because you said that made it easier."[75]

"Are you smashed?"

"Amy, I'm...."

"What?"

"Look, I know that was a rotten party but don't you remember how we felt at the Biltmore and in the rain under the overhang of the gym door above Paradise Pond?"

[74.] MN: But he didn't. Do you think he really wanted to? He would never let me take a "mulligan," only hit a "provisional" ball when I banged the sucker into the woods.

KN: I can't be sure. But I tend to think if he had come out with a proposal then, she would have turned him down. It would have been too late, too sudden.

MN: But maybe she would have agreed to "make out."

KN: Is that all you think about?

MN: That's seldom what I think about these days. "Making out's" for kids. Joe and Amy had long been potential baby makers—and they knew it. Joe and I talked about what can happen if you don't go "all the way," but put your thing so close to hers that.... Wait up! Another possibility! What if he took her home and called you? Proposed to you, right then, over the phone?

KN: I don't think he would have done that. Ever!

[75.] KN: She never mentioned a "dating blouse" to the FEMS. How arcane, yet kind of sexy. Sure, he may have stretched a blouse, but with the clock ticking he needed to come up with a more compelling memory. They had plenty.

She grabs the black iron rail and climbs past the lamp-post, feeling inside her mailbox before Joe can catch up.

"What are you doing?"

"I'm getting the key."

He wants to spin her out of her towel and out of her swimsuit. If a car passes or a light from inside floods them he doesn't care. If only she will listen. If only he can say the right words.

She inserts the key. "Thank you very much. You'll come to the church and to the party Carrie's coming home to give at Calhoun Beach? I think you'll like Larry. You're a lot alike. My parents might even like him if he weren't Catholic."

"You must remember our old stretched out dating blouse!"

"Thanks, Joe, for a nice time." She holds out a cheek. He kisses it, inhaling all he can before she pulls it abruptly away.

"I'll…I'll call you."

"That would be nice. You call. I'm going to be a lonely little girl for the next two weeks. But then it'll be *mucho* busy, *n'est-ce pas*?" He takes a step toward her, but she backs inside leaving only perfume, smoke, her brightest smile, and a tornado blasting through his gut.

Back in the car he releases the brake and coasts down her hill, turning left past the postal storage box she always banged with a stick, stopping at her alley. He doesn't get out to climb it. She will have left no messages in their hiding place behind the license plates. Bells may be ringing on the hill for Robert Preston and his Librarian, but tonight Amy didn't hear them. She didn't hear them at all. And—Amy used to hear them, longer and louder than anyone.[76]

---

[76] MN: Luther said, "Joe wanted to learn from Kathy and go to bed with Amy." I think he'd worked his way down to only one of those choices after that night. But what if, instead of thinking about banging the postal box, he'd turned his car around—or, hell, ran back up the hill, three house's for God's sake—and banged on her front door and really asked her? Do you think Amy would have broken her engagement?

KN: I'm guess I'm not really sure. God knows, I don't know.

MN: But God does know.

One Year Later—Fall '58

Joe runs into Frankie Hill in line at Hove's Market. While a little girl watches the boy bagging groceries, Joe tells Frankie, "I still think how terrific you were in the show! As Ed Sullivan would say if he'd seen you, 'Terrific! Really terrific!'"

"Thanks."

"You doing okay?"

"I'm doing okay. At first when you guys finished senior year and went off to college, I have to admit I'd drive by that wall at the end of Pleasant and find myself thinking, 'Wham, right into the concrete!' But I'm going to be fine. Just fine—maybe almost wonderful."

"I drove by one day and was going to stop."

"You should have. Mothering a little girl takes more out of you than tumbling. I haven't seen many people. I find myself listening to too many soap operas. But I appreciate what you did when you were around and what you would have been willing to do. It was a dream being up there with you: singing and dancing—feeling thin and in shape. They really liked it, didn't they?"

"They ate it up." He carries her bags. She takes the hand of the little girl. "She must be almost ready for school."

"She'll be five, December 10th."

"She's cute. And I hope you know how pretty you always look."

"For a single parent?"

"You never told Jeff did you? What did you name her?"[77]

"I named her Sally. But not for the new Sally in *Peanuts*. I found an apartment in Richfield and changed from St. John's. I think I'd had enough of Father Doyle. He became pretty severe. I didn't feel I had any choice back then, but now I'm so lucky to have Sally."

Close to her, even knowing what he knows, Joe has to admit an attraction remains, the tightening in his gut, the stiffening beneath his trousers.

"Tell me," Frankie says, "why did you ask whether I told Jeff? Did you mean Hatch? We stopped going out before *Midsummer Night's Dream*."

"I guess I guessed wrong. Sorry."

"You thought Jeff was Sally's father? Thank God, no. Although her father's not your usual boyfriend-type either. We didn't go out much. I know everyone thought he was kind of a screw-off, but he was kind and he was funny. Pretty far from the marrying kind, even if I'd given that a thought."

"I'm surprised."

"And curious?"

"Yeah. But don't tell me anything you don't want to."

"I call my girl Sally Hill, but that's not her real name."[78]

---

77. KN: Why a note here?
   MN: Probably don't need one. You go take a break. Probably don't need this scene.
   KN: Then cut it!
   MN: Probably will. You take a break.
78. MN: Name's really "Nolan."
   KN: I'm back and I don't believe you. Impossible! How do I know you're telling the truth?
   MN: You don't! But how do you know I'm *not*? Want to call in Luther? He dropped out of med school to become a lawyer, then senator, but he could do some blood work. Besides if you memorized the end of our Dedication—Footnote 15, Page 25—you'll recall I reminded you: "This is only a book."

Fourteen Years Later—
Christmas 1972[79]

Impressed by the bronze Atlas and this year's majestic pine from Washington State, Mr. Joseph Taylor stopped at the curb, envious of skaters swirling behind him. Traffic on Fifth Avenue kept him from crossing with his wife and daughter. Snowflakes hit his lip and the scent of chestnuts made him realize he'd never tasted one.

A cab sliced so close it splashed Lucy's once-shiny Mary Janes causing Mrs. Taylor to grab and carry her across the Avenue. The yellow bullet shot behind them and Mrs. Taylor turned to scowl at Mr. Taylor. He thought, "Beautiful day, well?"

Lucy looked in Sak's where children jostled for space to see miniature trains and blinking rainbow villages. She pulled her parents on to Best and Company's English Yule scenes.

---

79. MN: And this scene jumps ahead and isn't in Joe's Journal either. It isn't even in those JO sheets. Well, it's there, but the typing looks different.

KN: It's done by computer, dearie. Printed by a now quaint dot matrix. It's also a scene that you and I are seeing for the first time. We were both at the Excelsior picnic, summer of '57, and you hit golf balls with Joe at Hiawatha. But neither of us lived this last scene in New York with him.

MN: So, can you shut up and let me read it!

On the Avenue, in the richest and poorest village in the world, women wore vacation tans; models in heavy pancake brushed men in torn coats with bagged bottles; executives in suits and skirts shouted greetings on their way to working lunches. People strolled or sped everywhere, except those slumped in doorways holding tin cups. Joseph expected his family to grasp what "poor" meant, and Lord knows they knew about "rich." But could he ever expect them to under-stand what it meant to be Midwest Middle Class? What it felt like to loop eighteen holes twice a day with a heavy bag over each shoulder, then wait more than four hours each round to find out whether your men would tip you, and at night stretch to look in the clubhouse window at a Minikahda or White Bear dance.

Lucy had asked for fresh snow for Christmas and gotten it along with almost everything on her list. This snowfall might cover, or at least delay once again, his need to explain to his daughter how some people she had never met, and might never meet, actually lived.

Philya Buckley Taylor, member White Bear Yacht Club, Board of both MOMA and the Guggenheim, looked at home on Fifth or any glossy Avenue. Her liquid attention poured from sight to sight in front of gold and silver in Tiffany's windows. She had been taught well by Midwest parents who prided themselves on daughters like Philya and Cynthia: good girls who could captain a boat, spin a tennis ball, and prep out East.

Lucy broke away and skipped across an icy patch to where workers climbed scaffolds to sandblast the Cathedral. Pigeons hopped beneath the workers, mixing with veiled shuffling women.

Screaming cars blurted flat notes, yet subtle snowflakes and chestnuts dominated the din. Mr. Taylor reached for his daughter's hand, but missed. So he walked behind his wife's tailored coat, reminded that she grew up riding horses and growing hips a touch too horsy.

He called, "This year's tree traveled all the way from Washington."

Philya tipped her head to acknowledge what he knew she judged insignificant.

Lucy backed up the steps to the Cathedral doors. "I'm tired."

"We've plenty of time before we drop her at your sister's. I've never been inside St. Patrick's. Let's rest your legs. I bet they've saved a seat."

"A pew! And I bet they'll have plenty of empties at Lincoln Center too. Everyone saw *Oklahoma!* years ago and at every high school since."

Joe imagines Kathy calling, "Oklahoma, okay! Yeow!"[80] While Carrie might be calling from Virginia, "You blew it, Joe honey; I worried you would." And Amy? He isn't sure. He sees the dusty paint-cracked show curtain rising on sun that swims on the rim of a hill. As always Aunt Eller rocks and works her butter churn, arm lit by straw and amber gels. The conductor invites in more instruments as the cowboy tells Aunt Eller the corn's as high as an elephant's eye. Of course Joe knows that by now Laurey's in place behind the farmhouse flats waiting for her cue, motionless so she won't ripple the canvas.

Lucy's eyes followed the Cathedral toward the sky. "All those windows. Do they ever wash the colored ones?"

"Colored" caused Joseph to wince, but he wanted to toss her skyward, catch and hold her as tightly and gently as Hiawatha holds Minnehaha above the Falls back home.

"Don't go in there," Philya told Lucy.

"Why not?" Joseph asked. "We have time before the matinee."

Philya said, "Oh I suppose it can't hurt. I think of myself as tolerant, but this is a faith I've never been able to accept."

---

[80] KN: See, he does remember me. Oh, thank you, Joe dear!
MN: One line! Heavy!

Inside the portico Joseph gave Lucy a bill to drop in the velvet-lined collection box. Her fingers parted; the bill floated toward the slot. Before it disappeared she raced up the right aisle stopping at an alcove to stare at those kneeling to light candles.

"I want to do that too."

"We are *not* Catholic. Hardly anyone we know *is*."

"I don't see what harm it will do," Joseph said.

"All right. Take a stick from the sand. Light it from the closest candle."

"Why closest?" Lucy asked.

"Safer. I always worry about little acolytes with long surplices."

Farther down the aisle on their right, a dozen people filled the front pews facing a transept altar. A priest adjusted his microphone, lips moving soundlessly. Before him stood a teenage girl in an eggshell dress and a boy with polished purple lapels. Four girls in green stood behind them holding bouquets, their heights making their seemingly hacked-off hemlines an uneven stairway of knees. The microphone hummed. The priest gestured to an invisible assistant behind a column. Static crackled before the priest's voice settled into an indistinct murmur. The green girls knelt. Everyone knelt. The Taylors walked past.

Behind the magnificent central altar, the Taylors entered another chapel where Joseph imagined he saw faces from the skating rink. He wondered where they would all end: the tall tree hauled to the rink from Washington State, the couple starting from St. Patrick's.

Mr. and Mrs. Taylor followed Lucy back toward the microphoned priest and wedding party. "I guess she's somewhat pretty," Philya said. "That forehead tangled in curls, some sleekness of the natural athlete."

"Cynthia in her prime?"

"I doubt that. I can't see her face through her veil. Imagine standing there," Philya grimaced. "People coming and going."

The orchestra swells beneath the baritone. The woman churning butter smiles. She can picture Curly telling his girl about the beautiful morning, how they will travel in the surrey, what she will dream, what people will say. The woman knows how it will all work out. Curly and Laurey: just a love story. Joe and Amy? Well, once....

Philya asked, "Why didn't your friend Kathy ever marry?"

"I always assumed she would."

"Did she ever call herself Kate? That has more flare! She seemed nice enough. Not at all flashy. And coming from a family of redheads I shouldn't say it, but I remember her hair had that peculiar cast—like the inside skin of an orange."

The one time Joe does go back, he walks the Parkway up Tarrymore and down the curve of Luverne past her house. At the foot of her street he bangs a stick on the postal box before climbing the alley. He hesitates by a stucco garage with a shape that seems right.... Or does it? It has a shed like the one where she kept the Raleigh that she bucked him on when she bloodied her knee. No! The backyard fence angles the wrong way for her father's garden. He moves down the alley one garage finding lattice that did once enclose roses and a shed that she did lean against, giving them a few weeks of worry.

Joseph said, "Kathy never found the right person I guess. Not everyone does, God knows."[81]

Philya adds, "And that Southern girl: she seemed a bright hustling thing."[82]

---

[81] KN: "God knows." I have to give you that one, Mickey! You called that in Footnote 76, Page 200.

[82] KN: Opponents call Carrie, "Ms. Bright Lies Browne, Esq." As Culpeper County D. A. she gives Virginia a death penalty opponent in a death penalty state. As a Senator, Luther Stern is fighting that one to the death too.

"Why can't I go to the show with you?" Lucy asked. "Or get married here?"

"This is a day for parents. After we pick you up at Aunt Cynthia's your father will watch the Waltons with you, maybe M*A*S*H if it's not too violent, or if he's not winding down under his earphones from that rarefied atmosphere he shares with Joan and Jan and Lisa Kirk: all his Rodgers and Hammerstein girlfriends."

He wishes what they did not want to happen against her shed had happened. The one time Joe goes back he enters the shed, crossing through cobwebs. Their hiding place likely became a dead letter office more than a decade ago. He scrapes his knuckles feeling low on the wall behind the plates. And his fingers find an ancient Valentine. He takes it back to read by car light:

Amy—Her List:

> *Wedgwood, enuf, and Princess Anne or Something Silver—Heavy Ends.*
> *Blue for the Bridesmaids: K, L, and C.*
> *Replacement Pink Panties for those You Ripped and Charcoal Gray for You, with Vest and Striper tie.*
> *Something filmy in basic black for me to decide to wear or not to wear. A cottagey place.*
> *And a sweater stretched wide around the neck that we'll call a "sub" for my "dating blouse."*
> *Bells too, and you don't even have to buy those — they were always there, high on the hill;*
> *One or the other of us simply failed to hear them. We make mistakes—isn't that so?*
> *But one fine day when they start to pull it all away...*
> *...très mal de pays.*
> *You always said I had a hard time saying it, but*

I'LL ALWAYS LOVE YOU, J.T., Jr.
ALWAYS...no matter what....
        Amy J. (Forget the "F"—I have)

Joseph said, "Make it a big night! How 'bout we watch Mary Tyler and Newhart too? See what sheets Newhart's wife puts on that great bed this week."

"No, I don't! I've decided not to get married," Lucy said. "No point to it! Look! They're kissing. All 'messy-mouthed.'"

Joseph saw the smear of lipstick, heard an organ throb filling a long silence. "Messy-Mouthed": what they used to call "Kissy-Face."

Philya snatched a thread from Joseph's cuff. "Lucy's right. They *are* too young. They look silly in those rented clothes: insignificant amidst this splendor."

Lucy hugged a column. "Why do people want to do that?"

"I don't know, dear," her mother answered. "I wouldn't. Not here."

"Maybe not for the matinee," Joseph said. "But my Shakespeare teacher, wonderful guy named Miller, taught us that Romeo and Juliet were about thirteen. What's that...7th or 8th grade?"

"That's always struck me as nonsense! Neither she nor Ophelia for that matter had the maturity to engage in an adult relationship. And think how different our times are. Population explosion, technologies most don't understand, all those radicals. Study! Play a sport! They're what matter!"

"I suppose you worked a place or two up your squash ladder at the club this week?"

"Her eggshell dress may look short, but it's puffed out in front. That couple will produce by Easter. My God, fertility! Find us a cab."

"Kids have strong feelings and love can be one of them. Love can come along very early. Sure, you can dismiss it. You're under pressure to do that. You're pressured to pass it off as a first feeling that will return again and again. You're taught not to trust or believe in it. Some find though that it never returns as strongly—or at all—ever again."

"Well listen to him! Mr. Puerile Delusion!"

Mr. Taylor followed Lucy and his wife past grottos where people prayed and prayed.

"It doesn't matter," Philya said reaching the door and daylight. "We're getting more of that snow you wished for, honey. How gorgeous! Look, don't miss it."

Lucy batted at flakes, puffy and clinging like cobwebs. Joseph turned back to face the long nave and its wide transepts. He bowed his head, once more entering a private inscape.

The small blonde with the straw ponytail who toured with the last National Company waits behind the canvas farm door flat, about to enter. He cannot see or call to her. Cannot confuse her cue. He must wait patiently for this Laurey to bang out the screen door of the white house, pressing the sides of her skirt, tossing her hair ribbon, skipping toward the throb of trumpets, the bite and clip of drums. Toward him. Toward Joe.

Bowing again toward the high altar, Joseph Taylor, Jr. joined his family on the Avenue. Sure, he knew that Lucy *was* young and lovely, that Philya *could* tease or ignore him when she was concerned with herself. But that didn't hurt too badly. At least she didn't think too much about him too often or take him too seriously anymore. And he usually knew where she stood: solid as a tree.

But out there somewhere old friends *did* dream of Wedgwood and Princess Anne—and of places to hide messages behind license plates nailed low on garage walls. All of those he wanted to honor—or cry over—even though all of those had likely—long ago—become impossibilities.

Instead, he walked on, trying to glory in whatever straw or lemon might gleam anew in the haze of a beautifully painted morning.[83]

---

83. KN: Well, Joe, you got your Hamlet-Romeo story.
    MN: But neither of them fuckin' died!
    KN: Maybe that's more difficult to live with.
    MN: Staying alive?
    KN: That might be sadder—sweeter and prettier.
    MN: You said that before, Babe. Twice! So can I cut this note?
    KN: No, Michael, you may not.
    MN: So is that the final word you promised?
    KN: Almost!

"J. A."

Saturday, February 29, 1936 - Sunday, August 23, 1998

...always there in country matters...[84]

[84.] MN: Okay, I'll bite. Now we've got a JA to go with JO and Joe. And it sounds like some dame, one who didn't make it out of the 20th century. So who stuck her in here?

KN: Let's say this comes mostly from JO. With a likely okay from Joe, and my vote to include his tribute.

MN: And Mister Beaver too?

KN: Why not? Sentiment: sadness and memory are okay. When talking loss, why not make it unanimous? We'll count you and all the beavers too!

A Half Century Ago with Author (JO)... [85]

Not so long ago Minneapolis built a public library at 53rd and Lyndale where, sixty years ago when four, I'd walk two blocks on Fridays to stand on the corner next to what was then the Piggly Wiggly Market. I waited for the Bookmobile—a treasured arrival! And I treasured moving back to Minneapolis two years ago to sit down with the best teacher I had in twenty years of schooling, Louis Claeson: 11th grade Shakespeare, 1951-1952. And with the best newspaper advisor, Carl E. Carlson of Washburn High's *Grist*. Sadly, by then my writing mentors from college years and after, New York theater director *Milton Lyon* and lyricist and librettist *Michael Stewart*, were no longer alive to join in looking back.

But I've been fortunate, over a half century, finding collaborators, mentoring friends who let their good stuff drip into work until it's hard to tell who made what possible—even *posthumously*. Slightly older writers and composers: Peter Blue, David Brown, Puggy Balch Chiarella, Peter Dowell, John Eaton, Ron Fredrick, Clark Gesner, Bill Glassco, Theodore James, Brooks Jones, Bob Mulcare, Stevie Brown Porterfield, Jack Schlegel, Bill Semans, Z. *Taylor Vincent*, Bob Wentworth. Slightly younger activists and artists: Bruce Adler, Woody Cannon, Pres Covey, Remi Cruz, Harold Cutler, Holly DeCinque, Michelle Doucette, Barry Forman, Carolyn Jagger Friedman, Steve Gilbert, Peggy Hoagland, Tom

---

[85] MN: JO's smear—finally! I'd call that, sinister mine, one sweet fuckin' tuck!

   KN: All these folks on JO's list: I thank them warmly, every one. For the reasons JO and Joe did, as well as for traveling patiently through this book—if any readers managed that trip without throwing dingbats at our interruptions.

   MN: Dingbats?

   KN: That's what the gentleman at the print shop calls those pennant shapes they put at the start of each new season, like "Spring '52."

   MN: Oh, I knew that. And they weren't "interruptions," but the best parts. Ought to know, I actually *read* those cause I wrote 'em—lots of 'em!

Jewett, Bruce Johnson, Marsha Levy-Warren, Walt McClennen, Al Price, Tom Rawls, Paula Saillard, Mark P. Smith, Kay Stuntz, Sarah Tantillo, Peter Temple, Ted Weidlein.

Plus finding rocks that let you lean: Myrna Noodelman Abrams, Knight & Marge Alexander, Tony Alvarado, *Tom Bachman*, *Carlos Baker*, Nancy Norvell Ball, Roberto Barragan, Jane Beck, Loran Benson, *Herman Berg*, Scott Berg, Jerry and Judy Bergfalk, Ken Bergstedt, Dudley Blodget, Seymour Bogdonoff, *Les Bolstad*, Tom Boodell, Bishop Frederick Borsch, *Ernest Boyer*, *Frank Brady*, Pete Bredehoeft, Marvin Bressler, Don Bugdal, Leslie Buxbaum, Ellen Cannon, Hodding Carter, Ink Clark, *Maurice Coindreau*, John Cooper, Saul Cooperman, Megan Cosgrove, Bob Coulter, *The Reverend Rowland Cox*, Andy Crabb, Brad Craig, *George Christian*, *Burt Davies*, Ellen Davies, Jerome Davis, John Davis, Fred Deming, Lynn Anken Deming, *Paul Dickey*, Humphrey Doerman, Jean & *Tom Donlon*, Henry Drewry, Carl Drummond, Stu & Petie Duncan, Alden Dunham, Louise Dunham, *Jack Edie*, Phoebe Epstein, Eb Faber IV, Greg Farrell, *Carl Fields*, Dean Jerry Finch, Richard Flanagan, John Fleming, John Friedman, Al & Alyn French, John Gager, Karl Gajdusek, George Gallup, Jane Anthony Garneau, Fred Glimp, David Godine, George Goethels, Robert Goheen, Priscilla Pierce Goldstein, Jack Goodman, Huson & Mimi Gregory, Steve Gregory, *Richard Green*, Bill Grieder, *George Grimm*, Dean Groel, Sheldon Hackney, Hugh Hardy, Greg Harney, Nat Hartshorne, Dr. William Haynes, Bruce Hazard, Sister Maryann Hedda, *Frederick Hilgendorf*, Fred Hird, *Harold Hodgkinson*, Pharis Horton, Bill Howarth, Duncan & Barbara Hoxworth, Dick & Barbara Iverson, Tom Jamison, Tom Johnson, Lanny & Sarah Jones, Teddy Jones, Tom Kean, Mike Keeley, Virginia Kirshner, Ev Kline, Robert Krause, Jim Lane, Señor Don Larson, Dale & Peggy LeCount, Donn Leussler, Steve Lieberman, Bill Lockwood, *Harold Lundholm*, Gene Maeroff, David Mallory, Win Manning, Bob McKinley, Ted & Jennifer McLean, John McPhee, Bruce Merrifield, John & Connie Miller, John Milton, Lee Mitgang, Dick Moll, Franklin Moore, Hadley Nesbitt, *Rob Noel*, Jon Parsons, David Perham, Dr. Jerry Peterson, Dr. David Plimpton, Mary Pollard, Christopher Porterfield, Meredith & Nancy Price, *Nikos Psacharopoulos*, David Purpel, Dave and Susie Rahr, Wistar Williams Rawls, Carl Reimers, Rich Rein, Kim Rennie, Spencer Reynolds, Rochelle

Robinson, *John Rowe*, Bill Rust, Vickey Sailliez, Betty & *Laddy Sanford*, Kati Eriksson Sasseville, Jean Ann Schlegel, Charles Schultz, Marvin & Lulu & Jonathan & Carol & Noah & Holiday Segal, *John K. Sherman*, Bill Shinn, Heidi Shinn, Ted Sizer, Bob Sklar, Cindy Smith, John & Penny Solum, Jane Sommer, Bob Steffen, Don Stolz, Chuck Stone, Art Thomas, *Lawrence Thompson*, Herb Titus, Susan Toth, Kim Townsend, *Mel Tumin, Andrew Turnbull*, Jeff Walton, John Weingartner, Dan White, Laird & Reid White, Jim Wickenden, *Beverly Williams*, Gail Thompson Williams, *Tom Williams*, Jim Winn, Geoffrey Wolff, Kathy Werness Youngblood.

Although this work is fiction, what would beat a bag lunch, on either the boys' or girls' side of the cafeteria, with friends whose names sound like:[86]

Truman Abram, Ted Anderson, Sue Kent Axtell, *Pat Barnard*, Janet Swanson Barnes, Tom Bennett, John Bergstrom, Gretchen Urness Bieto, Gwili Olson Blair, Jim Blanchard, Sharon Selander Borrell, Gladys Turnbull Bowden, Patti Spanyers Boyd, Marilyn Recroft Brothen, Sally Wallace Brown, Morrie Brownstein, Bob Bugby, Betsy Campbell, Rosemary Ditzler Conroy, Del Duell, Bill Dyste, Bob Dyste, Charlie Edwards, Rick Fesler, Bob Frazer, Diane Solberg Getman, Sally Swanson Gleason, Mimi Graceman Gleekel, *Shelly Goldfus*, Betty Larson Gramer, John Grathwol, Natalie Grodnick, Barb Hall, Fred Hall, Carol Goulet Hammond, Dick Hansen, Judy Pommer Hansen, Sterling Hardy, Bob Hendrickson, Dodie Reque Holmes, Punkin Hartigan Hubbell, Barb Meyer Huso, Nancy Wagner Jenkins, Bunny Anderson Johnson, Mimi Johnson, Nancy Johnson, Brad Jones, Nancy Mickey King, Marvyl Nelson Kotsonas, Ron Kuffel, Dorothy Wittig Kunze, Eddie Langert, Cathy Knudtson Larsen, Dick & Margaret Bieswanger Leonard, Mac & Karen Lindsay, Gretchen Baily Littlefield, Marian Fairbanks Locke, Jeris Sando Loser, Rachel Melena Matzke, Marty Mayer, Gwen Jenkins McIntyre, Al Mogck, Judy Nyvall, Marilyn Nordstrom Olson, Helen Bergh Palmer, Pete Passolt, Marilyn Frost Pearson, Jerry Putnam, Sheila Glass Reback, Cindy Mandelstam Rosenthal, Jerry Schottler, Francie Hubbard Schulz, Sharon Halron Stickel, Jim Sutherland, Joyce Berthiaume Sutherland, Juanita Pattridge Swisher, Dick Tipping, Emily Walker Ulhorn, Jim Vieberg, Bonnie Safely Young, Ramona Schultz Zilka, Joe Zwak.

[86.] MN: I'm bailing out here, babe. Can't handle all these names. What do I care how many cats JO twiddled? If I stop here, I won't have to read your long promised "last word." Unless…you're sure you didn't toss that in with your poetic ending of the St. Pat's scene?
KN: Yup!

Or what beats working past midnight on a five-sided stage with do-what-it-takes enthusiasts whose names sound like:

Larry Anderson, Carol Barr, Liz Barrett, Allen Bowles, Donna Briggs, Sue Brown, Jennifer Burkett, Vicki Cameron, Dan Carter, Joy Child, Martha Child, Fran Cibel, Sue Clippinger, Harv Cobb, Barry Copp, Brian Copp, Jim Cryer, Charlie Cutler, Cynthia Davis, Judy Davis, Nancy K. Davis, Nancy W. Davis, Jan Debye, Bob DeNormandie, Craig Donaldson, Gordon Donaldson, Scott Emmons, Mike Farnum, Chris Filbin, Laurie Forbes, Carol Freund, Chappy Garrison, Barbara Jagger Giamatti, Sue Goodwin, Heidi Grey, Richard Hand, Charles Harris, Peggy Hatfield, Vi Heath, Ginny Hendrick, Louise Hendrick, Rich Hendrick, Electa Kane, Lynda King, Jerry Kramer, Sue Lawrence, Cherrie Loesel, Rocky MacFarland, Nancy Magazu, Leslie Miller, Melody Moir, Joyce Monaghan, Philip Moss, Nancy Newmann, Pat Palson, Martha Poole, Anne Remmes, Barbara Reynolds, Paul Rhodes, Linda Roehrig, Sally Rogers, Cynthia Smith, Martin Sweeney, Mary Tooker, Judy Travers, Nancy Turk, Sandra Vanaria, Dale Wasson, Carol Way, Philip Way, Kay Wilson, Marcia Wilson, Judy Wright.

Or stolen study time while waiting to start rehearsing with country day students with names like:

Mark Blaxill, Jennifer Chandler, Steve Cragg, Ibby Crothers, Creigh Duncan, Betsy Murdoch, David O'Connor.

Or a chance to teach grammar to your "brand new" English Master as an experienced 8th or 9th grader with a name sounding like:

Eric Canton, Josh Coburn, Scott Cooney, John Edie, Donnie Heng, Greg Hickok, Rich Kemerer, Dave Kittams, Jeff Lewin, Dan Lindsay, Chuck Lundholm, Sandy Pfunder, Jack Seed, Mugs Thomas, John Tobin.

Finally, thanks to design and art professionals Jack Caravela and Jaana Bykonich, not only for their technical craft, drawing, and niceness but also—paying Mickey's highest tribute—for their "go-fast" story ideas. To my publisher Beaver Adams, acknowledgment that I lucked out discovering his experienced guidance while gaining a treasured friend. Ancient bows to Laura Matthews for encouraging the 1,200-page monster of 1976 that contained the germ of *Country Matters*. Appreciation to Hinda Greenberg for a nudge to "write some" every day, and ditto to Yitzak Shnaps for wry reminders. Gratitude for the long haul loyalty of Jack Langguth, author of serious books about so much, who always found something to encourage in the nine finished but unpublished novels that preceded *Country Matters*. Admiration to Richard Peabody for seeing shape in the twin stories. Recognition to novelist Mary Gardner for her early reading, to Connie Anderson and Elizabeth Jones for editing, and to biographer Jack Koblas for a last reading. However: *after* their editing, whispers in the print shop indicated late revisions. So I accept responsibility for any errors—able to blame them, of course, on Michael Nolan.

And a toast to an irreplaceably fine family! In Bookmobile times—*Helen* and *Fritz, Haha* and *Andrew Merrill*. Today—Patty, Tom, and Chris.

Minneapolis, 2000

JO[87]

[87.] KN: Author JO asked me to thank you for all you did.

MN: Well? Are you going to?

KN: For "all the work you did, Michael"? That's another "did-s't he or didns't he" matter, isn't it? I'll have to think about that. Maybe.

MN: No matter. Listen up! Gotta mighty deep concept! If Joe's not a real person…only some fictional character….

KN: The Copyright Page makes that clear.

MN: And what if Author JO is also only a fiction?

KN: Possible.

MN: That leaves you—and me of course. The only real people! Except Gerta Stalacta who tossed the beer bottle on Highway 100.

KN: Check out Page 51. *Loraine Herring* broke the bottle. So how can you be sure that those girls are real? Or that *we* are?

MN: Tell me something! If your answer's "yes," you got royally ripped off by the publishers. That is *we* got ripped. Tell me whether you honestly believe your name belongs in the author's place on the cover? And if you do, doesn't that make the "Commentary" (funny as your crutches, right?) count for as much, *or more*, than the "Narrative" (sweet enough to gag a weight-watching humming bird)?

KN: Well, maybe.

MN: Shit, everyone's got a love story, whether or not they play out their role, but us twins came up with twin stories. So tell the truth! And here's how you can make sure to get that last word that seems to mean so much to you. Do you think *you*—rather than your sweet waffling neighbor Joe Hamlet—are really the book's main character? The truth now: do you?

KN: Maybe.

About the Author

Although raised in Minneapolis and a graduate of Washburn High, John Osander wrote most of *Country Matters* during forty years in the East. He earned degrees at Princeton and Harvard, and studied at Yale Drama, Macalester, Rider and the University of Minnesota. While away from the Midwest, he directed the Princeton University Admission Office, founded the first state Teacher Recruitment and Placement Office, and served at the Carnegie Foundation for the Advancement of Teaching as Senior Deputy to the President, a former U.S. Commissioner of Education. Returning to his Minneapolis roots, he lives, once again, not far from the fenced field and poplars of Washburn.[88]

About the Novel

As Kathy Nolan always knew and Joseph Taylor discovers, Juliet and Ophelia and their guys, indeed all teens, possess a power to love that's too serious to be taken seriously. It comes too soon, gets misunderstood, dismissed, treated as not quite trustworthy, not quite real."[89]

---

[88]. KN: You sound like a nice fella. Single? We've met, haven't we?
[89]. KN: Around the Twin Cities? Washburn? In a book…maybe?
   MN: Last word, witch!
   KN: …maybe?